I0550353

A TRUST EARNED

DIANA CASTILLEJA

Purple Sword Publications
Tucson, Arizona

A TRUST EARNED
Copyright © 2014 DIANA CASTILLEJA
ISBN 978-1-61292-108-2
ISBN 10: 1612921086

Cover Art Designed by Anastasia Rabiyah
Edited by Shoshana Hurwitz and Traci Markou

Published by Purple Sword Publications, LLC
Tucson, Arizona, USA
www.PurpleSword.com

Chapter One

Late Summer, Southwest Oregon

Bram looked over his shoulder and swallowed at the absolute certainty that he wasn't alone. A rustle of sound whispered to him from the trees, a movement beyond him hidden by the darkened shadows between trunks and foliage. Something he couldn't see but could hear was prowling, pacing him, unseen deep in the shadows. More than once, his gaze strayed to the brush and trees surrounding him. He did his best to ignore it as he walked. He'd had the invisible companion for the better part of a day and a half already. Whatever it was hadn't bothered him, and he couldn't see it. He was fine with the status quo.

Pausing for a break, he raised his canteen and took a short sip, capping it carefully when he was done. He was being cautious with his water, trying to not gorge himself on what was left. He didn't know when he'd find water again the way things were going for him.

He searched the dusky tree line with a straining gaze but couldn't see anything to give away the source of the sounds that had all but mimicked his every step. A soft breeze shook the trees and sunlight broke through the canopy overhead a moment later, arcing in slices of radiance and bringing the realization home that he was being foolish. He was alone in the woods except for Mother Nature, but it didn't stop the feeling of being observed either.

After a few minutes of studied scrutiny, he realized with a sense of dread that the shadows were thickening with evening closing in around him. Darkness was taking over the tree line and quickly obscuring his path. The unwelcome idea came to him that he was going to have to spend yet another night lost among the trees. With that fact looming, he was thankful he had brought his windbreaker on a whim, his only protective garment tied around his waist as he had made his way down miles of trails.

He cursed at his own arrogant stupidity as he slowly started to hike again. He'd gone much farther than he had planned, assuming with the aid of his compass and the recognizable landmarks that he could leave the main trail safely. That was the first mistake he'd made. The second was not having enough food for what he'd thought would only be a day hike. His father would have been ashamed at his brash overconfidence.

He clenched his fists as his father's teachings flooded him. He knew better. *He knew better!* He ground his teeth, fighting off a wave of despondency, an acute depression the death of his father had left in his life.

He took a calming breath, releasing it slowly, determined to center his thoughts. Realizing now that he had gone too far didn't do him any good, other than to drill home the fact that he was going to be sleeping on the ground one more night.

"Priorities," he muttered as he studied the landscape around him, hunting for the best place to bunk down. Rolling hills led to brief, sharp rises of low escarpments and trees. He spun and twisted to take in his surroundings; larger-than-life Douglas Firs on either side of the trail he walked. He caught the swift twitch of a chipmunk's tail, scurrying with intent and speed to a hiding place as he walked past.

He'd set out the morning before, full of enthusiasm, a happy anxiousness to visit the area where he and his father had camped together, had spent their last summer being a father and son before Bram had left for college. He'd been absorbed in the views, the peaceful abandon that wasn't possible in the middle of St. Louis. There was something spectacular about the land, a freedom, a scent in the air, the way he could stretch his frame in the wildness of the Pacific Northwest that even the best manicured park couldn't emulate. And he'd lost track of time.

He'd realized late yesterday that he'd also lost his compass. He could hear his father berating him for his carelessness. So now he was lost. He could've sworn he'd been positioned south of the Sisters, but he hadn't seen the twin mountain peaks through the tree line for a while and had become nervous as the day grew later, fearing that, as humans could do, he was walking in circles.

Bram stopped on the path, hearing faint sounds coming from the shadows. He slowly twisted his head, his gaze sharp, his ears tuned in to the natural hum around him. The snap of a twig. The flutter of leaves settling. The hairs on the back of his neck stood up.

"Who's there?" he called, subconsciously aware it was only him and nature, and Mother Nature didn't talk. He narrowed his eyes as he searched into the shadowed, twined undergrowth. He shook his head, forcing himself to relax. No, there wasn't anyone else here, just him and a lot of small, furry animals.

Pushing away the wary feeling, he looked up, craning his neck to get a better idea of where he was, but the path was narrow and the coverage was high, already casting long shadows before him. He should have tried to find a place to bed down for the night over an hour ago but he'd been determined to find his way out of the woods, and now he was short on light.

He continued in a direction that he hoped was correct, using lengthening shadows to guide his steps. Several minutes later, he broke through the edge of the trees to find a gentle clearing with an earthen mound to the side. He hated the idea of lying out in the open another night, praying the occurrence of predators was still rare in this particular area of the state. Then, he scowled as the thought occurred that he didn't really have much of a choice considering the lessening light.

Making a circuit of the clearing, he checked for recent prints or signs of life. After two circles and finding nothing that would be alarming, he bundled a few twigs with fallen limbs and dug a shallow pit with the heel of his boot, putting the small hill of dirt at his back. Thankful he had remembered to put his travel lighter in one of the windbreaker's pockets, he used it to start a small fire for a little light and a touch of warmth. It was a barrier more than a bonfire.

He crossed his arms to lean against the grassy knoll, long legs stretched out before him beside the smallish fire. He loved to hike, to be outdoors. His original plans had actually been to hike Yellowstone but on his way west, he'd changed his mind. He'd already been through miles of Yellowstone. He and his brother Mitchell had made numerous trips to the well-known parklands with their father while growing up, but their last trip together had been special. He hadn't known it and neither had his father, but it would be the last camping trip they would ever take together.

Their father had been a real woodsman, a throwback. He could hunt, fish, and camp like a pioneer. No matter how long he lived in the city, his father had never lost his wonder of the great outdoors.

While Bram hadn't received that entire gene, he was happy to learn. He had survival knowledge, could tell direction by the stars and if necessary, could find a way to eat and stay alive. He silently prayed it didn't come to that on this trip. Eating bugs had never been a secret childhood fantasy, even though his dad had shown him how to do it and to be able to look beyond what he was consuming.

The thought made Bram smile softly as he stared at nothing, his thoughts lost on the past. Man, he missed his dad. He was the reason he'd come out west. His death had been unexpected and difficult. This trip was for him. Homage to the man and what he'd loved, a memory to his skill. His mom and Mitchell were still at home, starting to rebuild. She was starting over, and Mitchell was starting college. They had all tried in their own way to make peace with his passing, but it hadn't been easy. They never once thought he'd get cancer and never doubted he couldn't beat it.

He reached for the canteen at his side and took a shallow swallow, shaking it with dejected expectancy. He frowned. Less than half. He was going to have to be careful with what he had unless he could find fresh water.

He canted his head, looking up to search stars starting to dazzle the darkening night sky. He sought the patterns that he'd learned when he was a boy, sitting on his father's knee in their own backyard. He located north, then made the compass in his mind's eye, finding south and east, then relaxed. He could find his way in the morning.

Content for the moment, he was staring into the fire when he heard a sound, like a soft sneeze from out of the darkness. Hunting the tree line he didn't find anything, yet as his gaze coursed back and forth, the hairs on his neck stood up with little warning. There was that feeling of being watched. His lips thinned. He knew he was tired, and by morning his ignorable hunger pangs would be as loud as the rumble at Busch Stadium during the playoffs, but the feeling that he was being watched would not leave him.

Staring into the shadowed depths, his gaze skipped and his breathing hitched to a hard halt. It wasn't at the tree line. It was deeper in the blackness. Two gray eyes, shining in the scant firelight with as much intent as he was watching them.

For a matter of heartbeats, neither so much as flinched. Then, in a blink, his watcher disappeared. He didn't move. He didn't breathe. When it looked as though whatever it was wouldn't be returning, he hissed the breath he had been holding. The encounter left him unsettled and wary for the rest of the night. He managed a stilted sleep at best, uncertain of where his midnight watcher had vanished to.

The next morning, feeling groggy and gritty, Bram refilled the hole his meager fire had made then, finding his directional bearings from his surroundings and memories of the stars the night before, aimed south. *Day three,* he thought the moment his stomach rebelled with a harsh sound.

He cursed again, not so silently this time as he trudged on a path that he hoped was *an actual path.* What would happen if he really was lost? According to his stomach, he'd allowed himself to go soft while in school. His long, grueling hours serving his internship at St. Louis Med Center in the ER didn't equate to long hours of actual exercise, and his stomach was letting him know it. He fought down the hunger pangs, making his feet move with purpose.

Unfortunately, thinking of the hospital, his other home, brought to mind Rebecca, the one person he was really trying to not think about too much while on this trip. She was making loud marriage noises, and he wasn't ready. He did care for her. At least, he assumed he cared for her. He imagined he could even be in love with her.

He shook his head even as he thought it. Something simply wasn't right between them. He had envisioned a life of love and happiness, like his parents had shared, but Rebecca didn't seem to be the right one. He could admit he cared for her, but he knew he wasn't happy anymore. He pushed a low-hanging branch out of his path. It was a feeling that as he'd progressed and picked his future they'd outgrown one another, but she refused to let it go. To let him go.

As his thoughts rambled, his feet carried him down one nonexistent trail to another, as due south as he could discern. He'd worn the windbreaker overnight to ward off the chill of the evening, a steep contrast to the heat of the days.

Oregon was in the middle of a hot streak. The day he'd left, it had been ninety-seven with forecasts of gradually increasing heat. Today it could be a hundred. He wouldn't have been surprised, but the jacket was beginning to impede his progress as branches and stiff growth grabbed at him. He took a steadying breath as he slowed, trying to refocus his attention to where he was putting his feet before he fell face first.

Giving up on the endless circling of his thoughts, he stopped to lean against the trunk of a tree to take a drink. The canteen was nearly empty now and as the sun broke through the trees, the predictions for the heat index looked like they were going to be scarily accurate.

Putting one foot in front of the other, he froze when he heard a rustle in the foliage to his right. It was louder, as if to acknowledge his presence. He peered into the trees in the direction it had come from but saw nothing. Sunlight and shadow.

He remembered the eyes from last night and felt a tingle on his skin. Something *was* following him, but when silence continued to be his only companion, he started walking again. He stopped shortly after to remove his windbreaker, wiping an arm across his damp brow. As much as he hated to do it, he drank the last swallow from his canteen. He frowned, aware that his options had shortened dramatically.

The sun had risen higher still, nearing its height when he noticed a change in the thickness of the trees. He cocked an ear, straining to listen beyond the normal sounds of nature. A stream or creek was to his left. He perked up with a hope of fresh water at hand. He followed the faint gurgling sounds for several minutes, finally breaking free of the trees to find a shallow, swift-paced creek.

Even as hungry and thirsty as he was and with his exhaustion growing, he could relish the beauty of what he had found. Bleached rock framed the waterway on either side, showing it was a winter runoff stream. Trees, tall and full, swayed on either bank in unison. It was a gorgeous spot. The water ran clear and cool when he knelt on the bank to test it. He drew one long, cleansing breath, savoring the crisp taste of the air on his tongue. His father had always said he'd had a good nose for the outdoors. Now he could understand what that meant.

He recognized the smell of the trees, the earth beneath his body, the scent of wildlife somewhere out of reach. He let his head drift to his chest, the feeling of his father and his words right there in his mind. He'd never allowed himself the release to cry at the funeral, and he had not cried when his mother needed him to be the man of the house. In this place of nature that was so much of what he remembered of his father, he couldn't hold back the pain, and he didn't even try.

His first sob was harsh in the quiet of the creek, a breaking that had been held in check for too long. The tumbling sound of the water was the only backdrop to the sharpness of his grief. Whether the freedom to finally give himself this moment was from emotional or physical exhaustion, it didn't matter. This place, this serenity, was who his father was, had been. For a brief moment the boy inside mourned his father like a son should, letting the empty space created by his death fill with memories and the love they had shared. For now, in his silent, private world, his show of grief was allowable.

Several minutes passed before he could take a steadier breath. The scent of this place would stay with him forever, helping him to remember his father. He unclenched his hands and wiped the tears from his eyes, having permitted his heart to finally bleed for the father he'd never talk to again.

Straightening to rest on his calves, he surveyed his surroundings with lengthening resolve and a deeper calm. Now he needed to get out of the woods. He leaned over to run a hand through the water. It was clear and cool, nearing cold. *Probably spring water this time of year,* he mused as the water drifted over his fingertips. Cupping his hands, he took a shallow, careful sip. All he tasted was a slight iron bitterness but nothing he couldn't handle. He slowly drank as much as he could on an empty stomach, then filled his canteen. With that done, he splashed his face, cleaning the emotional tracks and dust, scraping the excess water off with his fingers and shaking them dry.

Resting on his haunches, letting the sun beat down on him and absorbing the warmth rather than dreading the hours still ahead, he heard it. A click against stone, a movement, and the soft sound of...panting. He glanced over a shoulder and was stunned into stillness.

There in broad daylight, not more than fifteen feet away, stood a wolf. A beautiful creature of color and grace. They regarded each other, cautious but curious.

Wolves were not common outside of Yellowstone and he'd heard of no sightings this far west, but there she stood. He was positive it was a female. A slight build—a runner's body was the first thought that came to mind—and delicate facial features ending in a pointed snout. Inquisitive gray eyes that stared at him in equal fascination.

The remarkable thing about the creature was its coat—a blended near-white color with rough patches on her shoulders of golden yellow and yellow-tipped ears.

His heart raced. He was unable to move even an eyelash as the wolf raised its head, scenting the air with tentative actions. He continued to watch in awe until it whipped around and disappeared into the woods flanking him. He carefully turned in a crouch, listening for any signs it was still there, but the silence was deafening until he let out the strangled gasp he had been holding.

Holy crap! A wolf! He jumped to his feet, wondering if there were more, a pack. They hunted in packs, but somehow, he knew he was not in danger being more a curiosity to the animal, as it had been to him. He stepped toward the tree line, wanting to follow, to see if there were others. He stopped himself, shaking his head ruefully. He was lost and needed to keep moving if he was going to reach his car this century. He needed civilization, food, and a hot shower before he needed to find a lone wolf in the surrounding wilderness.

He looked once more, longing in his heart, curiosity on the tip of his tongue, but reluctantly, he acknowledged he couldn't. Facing the rushing creek again, he judged the flow and hoping it was going south, decided to follow it until he had to make another decision.

Hours later, he was frustrated and angry with himself all over again, starving, and ready to lie down and let whoever was able find him. The stream had disappeared underground several hours ago, and now he was blindly walking.

Where was he? How did he get so lost? He should have found some trace of a trail or a path by now. He cursed loudly when he realized that he was as lost this evening as he had been that morning. He pushed on, drinking from his canteen when the hunger became unbearable. Unfortunately, he was draining his water because of it.

He grumbled and cursed, positive he had somehow managed to walk in circles for another day. Even if he wasn't, he couldn't be this lost!

He sank down onto a felled tree, planting his head on crossed arms. He barked a shallow laugh. No one would even think of looking for him for another ten days. His vacation was for two weeks, and he'd only been gone for not quite four. He looked up, searching for the sun. Okay. Four. He was going to have to find a place to sleep again.

Exhausted, he rested. He'd set a frenetic pace since leaving the creek, wanting to get to a hot shower and a good meal. Yet as he sat, his stomach starting to touch his backbone, he realized his mistake too late. He was exhausted, weary, and hot. He sipped on his water, feeling the lighter weight of the canteen as he beat himself up over his mistake.

He stopped drinking before the urge to drain it became unbearable. No food in almost three full days of serious hiking. At least he wouldn't miss the gym for a while.

A flash of white caught his attention as he lowered the canteen. He blinked, rubbed his eyes, then dismissed it. He wiped the sweat from his brow, trying to clear his vision when he saw it again.

It was back, or maybe it had never left him. He wasn't sure, having paid less attention to his surroundings at the pace he'd set.

As he felt the heat of the day fall on him, he wondered if his imagination was working overtime. Weren't there legends about visions? Maybe he was having one, in the middle of Oregon.

Bram almost laughed. He was starting to lose it, too. *Great.*

He capped the canteen and didn't move. He was hot and achy. Starving was another fact. The flash of white streaked by again, beyond the nearest trees. Rubbing his eyes harder, he was surprised to find it still there, only it had stopped, blurred by shadows. He could barely make out the tail, like a white banner spotlighted by the fading light of the pending sunset. It twitched once when he stood. He didn't move again in case it bolted, but instead, it seemed to...wait. Disbelief had him shaking his head.

What did he have to lose?

"I know I'm imagining this. Do you want me to follow you?" he asked quietly, no longer concerned with who thought he might be nuts. The tail twitched at the sound of his voice. The animal didn't move, but he heard a distinct click. He cringed when he realized it had snapped its jaws at him. "I am going crazy," he muttered as he carefully followed the retreating tail into the trees.

He didn't know how long he followed it or how far he had traveled when he discovered they'd stopped in a clearing. As the animal blended into the foliage at the next line of trees, he realized with a feeling of wonder that he was standing at the top of the trail. At the very least, a trail he knew he could follow. He spun on a heel looking for the wolf, only to find he was alone. The wolf was gone.

He searched, half hoping that somehow it would still be there, but knew even as far as visions went, he shouldn't be looking for it at all. Accepting that he had found a way out, he dug a pit and made another small fire, doing it the same way he had the night before and on more nights over his life than he could count. He settled down close to the little beacon of light, ready to make the march in the morning for civilization, when there was a stirring in the trees opposite.

He lifted his head, the dark line of the trees becoming impenetrable in the falling darkness. Cautiously, the wolf moved forward, a limp form clutched in its jaws. It dropped the rabbit carcass several feet from him, then began to back away. Gray, luminous eyes watched him intensely.

"Wait!" he whispered, unsure why he did or if it mattered. He realized he was imagining all of this; he had to be. The wolf froze at the sound of his voice. Then it sat on its haunches and stared at him. "Why are you here? Are you a vision? A dream?" He swallowed thickly as the animal tilted its head, listening to him. It clicked its jaws at him again with a raw snap.

He smiled at it, not in the least concerned. Visions weren't real. "Sorry. Not my language." It appeared to him that the animal smiled in return as it gracefully stood. In the distance, there was a howl, long and deep.

It caused a shiver to race over his skin. He watched with acute fascination as the one before him lifted its head and answered with a long soulful sound that reverberated through the night and filled him with wonder.

Without another glance at him, it slipped into the trees. "Thank you, my white beauty," he said into the darkness. A faint yip reached him on a breeze, then there was silence.

Chapter Two

Six years later

"Paging Dr. Benedetti. Paging Dr. Benedetti. Please call extension two-four-one."

Bram Benedetti barely lifted his head at the summons, his gaze intent on the chart he held in his hand. When he addressed his patient, his smile was warm. "Mr. Logan. You're ready to be released. Is your daughter coming to get you?"

Mr. Logan returned the assessment of his favorite doctor, saying with aplomb and barely disguised hopefulness, "I wish you and Phyllis got along better."

"Sorry. My bedside manner doesn't have to include family members," he returned with an easy smile. *And not for cupid-intending fathers, either.* He didn't allow his thoughts to be revealed. "If you have any problems, make sure you or she contacts me immediately. I don't want to see you in here again for something as simple as a missed dose flare-up. Understood?" He wrote his recommendations down on the chart as Mr. Logan slipped from the exam table.

"I know. I know. It was my fault anyway."

"I understand." Dr. Benedetti's words were patient for Mr. Logan. It wasn't the first time he'd mentioned his unwed daughter. "Take better care of yourself, will you? I like the money, but don't make me charge you if I don't have to."

Mr. Logan's expression lightened. Bram knew that was one of the things Mr. Logan liked about him and why he always tried to get him to ask his daughter out. The patient came first.

Mr. Logan shook his hand. "That I can understand," Mr. Logan replied.

"Paging Dr. Benedetti."

"I need to get that. Goodbye, Mr. Logan." Leaving the exam room to answer the page, Bram dropped the chart off at the nurse's station and picked up the plain white auxiliary phone on the station desk. He slipped his pen into the pocket of his whites with an unconscious move. "Dr. Benedetti."

"Bram. It's about time. I was on hold forever. Why didn't you call me back? Just because we're divorced doesn't mean you can drop me like a damn container for refuse."

He cringed as soon as he heard the voice on the other end. The tension knot he'd almost forgotten about between his shoulders reappeared, and it brought relatives. "Rebecca, now isn't the right time for this. I'm on duty." He rubbed the tired spot between his eyes.

"Well, when will it be the right time? Tell me that?" she sniped.

He held his temper in check as he told her, "We are divorced. As in not married. Can't you let it be?" He fought to keep the tired edge out of his voice. His exhaustion had always been a weakness for her to attack him on.

"No. You know we never should have divorced. You know I still love you."

He bit his tongue. Even if Helen wasn't looking at him, she could easily hear every word, and the nurses gossiped worse than crows.

"Rebecca, I will call you this evening."

"You had better," she said, followed by a crisp snap and the welcome death of a silent line.

He shook his head at the phone, then set it down like it was a sleeping snake. "Helen, I'll be in my office checking messages. Page me if anyone other than Rebecca calls."

"Yes, doctor," she replied crisply.

He turned away from her and the subtle chaos of the nurse's station. The white light of the hallways meant nothing to him these days as he cut a path through the working environment. The sound of the carts, the rasp of ventilators, the smell of cleaners and antiseptics. It was ingrained now. After more than ten years of school, internship, and finally his own office with a plaque on the door in the same hospital where he had completed most of his training, it had ceased to have an effect on him. Any of it. And he wasn't sure what to do about it.

He sank into his office chair with a tired sigh, seeing the message light on his phone. He knew it had been too much to hope that she hadn't called him there as well. When he checked, there were five messages total. Two, of course, were Rebecca. He erased those without even wanting to hear them in their entirety. He couldn't blame her. He had been the failure, at least emotionally. He had never gotten beyond his original attraction to form something deeper. He had never been able to love her, not the way she had wanted or deserved.

Their divorce had been amicable at best. She hadn't wanted it but realized he'd been miserable. She had relented, probably believing giving him an easy out would show him what she really meant to him. She'd been wrong. Now, she'd become obsessive again, exactly like when they'd been dating, wanting what she couldn't have because he knew he didn't want her. He'd made a mistake and had paid for it.

One of the other messages was from his brother, Mitchell. They had grown closer after their father's death, and both brothers had become a stronger support for their mother when she'd needed them at her side. That time was gone but they were still tight as a three-person family, a healed family able to move on without his father.

He was reaching forward ready to dismiss the last message when it started to play. The voice, then the words, stopped him.

"Dr. Benedetti, my name is Selene Aiza. You don't know me, but I live in Oregon and recently worked with a colleague of yours who gave a very high recommendation for a position we are seeking to fill. I work in Bend, Oregon at the medical center, and after an exhaustive search would like to discuss a position with you. If you are interested in the details, please call me at..."

He leaned back. Oregon? Bend? He hit replay and listened again. The voice was feminine, soft and clear. His eyes drifted shut as memories of Oregon came to him. The smells, the beauty, the trails.

The wolf.

He blinked, startled as the image crystallized with vivid clarity in his mind. He hadn't thought of the animal or the incident in years. Had it really happened? Or had it been a delusional case of hunger and heat?

He shook his head, disrupting his thoughts. He was sure he had hallucinated it all. By the time he had made his way to where he had left his vehicle, he had been in the woods for four full days with hardly more than a canteen of water and his energy bars.

He lifted his pen out of his pocket and wrote down the number, listening to the message again to ensure he had it correct, then erased it along with the others. He stared at the name and the phone number for several minutes. He knew the important questions could only be answered by calling.

But what about his personal questions? What about his intentions, his own desires?

He rubbed his eyes to clear images and memories. The tension knot between his shoulders was still there, but it was lessening now that he'd had a few minutes of quiet time. When had that become necessary? When had the stress become such a normal part of his day that he could ignore it? Simply live with it, like the watch he wore on his wrist?

He loved what he did. The hospital he worked in and with was as much his home as the house he lived in, but in the last two years, something had become obvious. Like his relationship with Rebecca, it was no longer a good fit for him.

Frustration had become a normal part of his everyday life. Meetings and conferences were turning into long periods of grandstanding, where only a small amount of time was used for actual discussion of medicine. And the mere idea of Rebecca, or the mention of her name, was enough to make his stomach sour. He never should have allowed himself to be convinced by her to settle, because there was no doubt now with time and distance, he had. In that, he most certainly was to blame.

One thing he could remember about that wayward trip with marked vividness was the peace he had found while walking through the wilderness in southwest Oregon. Even when he had been lost, the splendor, the untouched quality, had filled him with a peace that he remembered in detail but hadn't found since.

Was he ready to make a change? If the opportunity was there, in Oregon, was he capable? There was only one way to find out.

Taking a chance, he lifted the phone and dialed the scribbled number. The other end answered on the second ring. "Bend Medical Center."

"Yes. Is Selene Aiza available?"

"Let me check. Who may I say is calling?" He gave his name and waited patiently when he was put on hold. He tapped his fingers lightly to the music playing into his ear. He didn't have long to wait.

"This is Dr. Aiza." Her voice was clear and lovely, better than the recording.

He introduced himself, saying, "I'm returning your call. You didn't leave much on the message."

He heard flowing laughter in her voice. "I was hoping saying nothing would be more intriguing than saying everything." He settled into his chair as she continued. "The reason I called was because of a friend and mutual colleague, Dr. Ross Spinitti. He worked with you for several years, if I remember correctly."

He smiled as he remembered Ross. Tall, lanky, and gregarious, but a good doctor. "Yes, I do remember him," he said. "I worked with him during my internship and, I want to say, until two years ago."

She murmured an agreement. "I believe that is how he described it. He thought very highly of you, and I can assure you, the board thinks very highly of Dr. Spinitti, but that is only to break the ice. The position we have requires a person with certain skills, knowledge, and capabilities that our hospital is singularly in need of. The board knows you are specialized in hematology, and that is also being viewed as an asset for our location." She hesitated briefly as if unsure of his reaction. "I know this is completely out of the blue for you, but you are the board's first choice."

"It is, at that," he answered. "Being out of the blue, that is." He looked around his office and felt the caged feeling that until that moment he hadn't bothered to acknowledge. There had been no sign of escape, until now. He pushed himself into his chair, relaxing further as he crossed his feet at the ankles.

"Tell me something?" he asked, an odd feeling starting to curl through him. It almost felt like anticipation. Maybe...even a hint of wonder. An element that had been missing for far too long.

"Anything."

"Is Oregon still as beautiful as it was six years ago?"

Her bright laughter was contagious, and he smiled.

"Gorgeous. I love it here. I couldn't picture living anywhere else."

"Why don't you give me a better idea of what this position is, Dr. Aiza, and I will let you know."

"Well, a good point for the position is that it isn't hectic, for starters. We do service the entire Cascades area and serve as an overflow center, but that happens only rarely. We do our own lab work, even for being a smaller community center and are well staffed and strong on equipment. The position is basically a co-directorship with minimal administration duties. We are searching for a specific kind of personality, a singular individual." Her voice dropped a little, a serious undercurrent to show her sincerity. "I know you've been at home in St. Louis, but the feeling is like nowhere else. And the pay is only a little lower than your current levels."

"You know what I make?" he asked, surprised to hear it.

She sounded apologetically embarrassed. "I had to do all the research on you, Dr. Benedetti. Please don't be offended."

He smiled as he envisioned her, a light blush rising on the imagined picture of her face from the confession. "How could I be? Your honesty is transparent."

"Thank you," she said. "So, could I interest you in a tour?"

He lifted a glance at his calendar, relaxing more as he shifted in his chair. He was off duty in two days. "Why don't I fly out on Thursday? Is that time enough?"

"I think we can manage for that. I hope we can entice you to call Bend home."

His laugh was light for the first time in years. "I'm willing to see."

* * * *

Bram's phone rang Wednesday night as he finished packing for his morning flight. He lifted it distractedly with a shirt in his other hand. He was relaxed until he heard her voice.

"You forgot to call," she reprimanded him crisply.

"Rebecca." He sighed, his gaze flowing upward, begging for divine intervention. *Any* intervention. He'd even take a lightning bolt at this point. "I'm sorry. I had emergencies for eight hours straight. I couldn't drop it all." He put the shirt on the bed as he sat.

"And what was wrong with now? You couldn't think of me at all?"

He grimaced at her fishwife mentality. Had she always been this demanding, this self-centered? If she had, then he had obviously been too easy. He silenced his groan of self-disgust.

"I'm leaving in the morning. I'm packing, and I hadn't really thought about it."

"Packing?" Her voice rose in a shocked cry. "Where are you going?"

He refrained from throwing the clutched phone at her outburst. "Jesus, Rebecca! What do you want from me? I don't have to tell you every single thing in my life!"

Her silence grew and spread like a wet cloud. "I'm sorry. I know we're divorced. I do still love you." Her meek words were a repetitive cover-up that he had learned was a short-lived respite.

"I can't help that anymore." His voice chilled, no longer interested in appeasing her. "I told you months ago there would be no reconciliation."

"Bram, please." She entreated in that helpless tone he had learned to hate. She was anything but helpless.

"No. Move on. Leave me out of it. My life is of no concern to you anymore. If I ever really was."

"What's that supposed to mean?" she demanded, all signs of meekness gone.

He stood from the bed, the hand holding the cordless phone pinched white from anger, pain, and stress. "Never mind. Forget I said it." He butted his head against the solid door frame to his room once, twice. Taking a deep breath to gain some type of control, he told her, "I have to go. I need to finish packing."

"All right," she offered, returning to playing the meek card. "Will you call me when you get back?"

He stood staring at the emptiness of his bedroom. There was nothing left for him in that room, as much as there was nothing left for him in St. Louis. His life was moving forward. It was time he actually did the same. His voice was final when he answered her.

"No." And he hung up the phone.

He dropped it onto his bed with a furious flick of his hand, picking up the shirt he had abandoned for the phone call. He folded it with precise movements, laying it with the half dozen others already in place.

He shook his head in anger and self-incrimination. Why had he married her? She was not the woman he was made for, no matter how much she wanted to be. He knew that. Hell, he thought sarcastically, he'd *known* it, and he'd still married her. So, if not her, then whom? He honestly didn't know.

He was successful, hard-working, good looking, or so he believed, but not conceited. His brother was far better looking and easier to be around. He had worked long hours and longer years to be a respected hematologist. He had been on more committees than he could remember decoding the connection certain blood diseases and conditions had to the development of cancers. Cancer like the one his father had died from.

Rebecca had never understood his dedication, his ambition. She had chased and cajoled, offered, and pleaded until he had given in and given up, and that weakness had been his downfall. She didn't understand the long hours of commitment. She didn't care if someone had to wait for her petty foibles. Once they had married, she had expected him to be her husband, not a couple, and definitely not a man with a career to answer to.

They had dated for two years, had been married for over two, and now were divorced for over a year, and she still thought she could order him around, that she could control him. He blinked as it sunk in. Six years. Had he really put up with her for so long?

He huffed a disgusted sound. Why? When he had known his feelings, his own heart and mind? He sighed, shaking his head at his thoughts. Because regardless of how much of a pain in the ass she was, he had cared enough to not want to hurt her. He had never wanted to hurt her inside. He folded a pair of slacks, taking care with the crease points, only paying attention to his packing with half a mind as his thoughts wandered from her phone call to what lay ahead. Two of his suit jackets hung in a carrier on the hook inside his closet door, and he was nearly done packing by the time he had lowered his blood pressure.

Thinking about his coming trip, he felt that rush of anticipation, like during his conversation with Selene Aiza. He was flying to Bend, Oregon. A small-town community with an even smaller center, which had a place for him. Maybe. He still needed to investigate it. Maybe it was time for a change. Maybe he was finally ready for one.

He loved St. Louis, loved to watch the Cardinals take it out of the park and pray with everyone else that the Rams would make the Super Bowl. He sank down to the edge of the bed lost in his thoughts, picking apart a few truths. How long had it been since he'd even done something as decadent as attend a baseball game? How long had it been since he'd drawn a breath and not felt caged, pressured, and in Rebecca's case, hunted?

His eyes drifted closed as the memories of his hiking trip from so many years ago returned. Green firs, rushing creeks. Beautiful sunsets and gorgeous sunrises not blocked by towering skyscrapers or overshadowed by the noise of life in the big city. The sweet smell of the wild country. His chest swelled as he inhaled, mentally reliving the moments of six years past.

He had set out again after his first wayward adventure of becoming lost. He had purchased another compass and, with food in hand, had resumed his tackling of nature, hiking for several days up and down trails.

He hadn't seen the wolf then, either. *The wolf.* He shook his head in logical denial.

A white beauty of an animal that had somehow, probably, saved his life. The memory still held the feeling of unreality, a vision or a dream. He had wandered, hungry and thirsty, when it had appeared almost as if from out of nowhere. Wolves were intelligent, but not so intelligent as to guide a human to safety when their first instinct was to avoid them if at all possible. How could a wild animal even *know* to lead him to a trailhead to begin with? He shook his head. It was an absurd mixture of unreality and vision. It had to be.

He had convinced himself as the days had passed without sighting the beautiful animal that he would have found the trail on his own. Yet he'd silently admitted, at least to himself, how far off the beaten path he'd been. He could have wandered another day or two, easily, before he'd realized that he was going in the wrong direction. The wolf had led him nearly due east when he remembered he had been determined to go southward, and the distance had been immeasurable. He probably would have hit northern California before finding any path that led him into the parklands he had intended to walk.

From somewhere deep in his memory, the smell of roast rabbit entered his senses and his mouth watered, almost as if the fire was right there and he could reach out a hand to touch the warm, cooked flesh, to taste it. That was the part that argued the vision theory. The wolf had killed it for him, of that he was sure. Why else would it have brought it? How else would he have even eaten? But it boggled the mind. Wolves *did not* feed humans. They did not *save* humans. He couldn't find a single explanation for what had happened that evening. Until that moment, with it all crashing into his memories again so clearly, he hadn't really tried. His hand shook with a gentle tremor where it rested on his thigh. He curled his fingers, forcing restraint. Steady breaths helped to turn the memories to mist.

He hadn't spoken of that encounter to anyone, not even to his brother, whose experiences equaled his with the great outdoors. He was sure Mitch would've loved to pick the whole episode apart, trying to convince Bram he had imagined it all. It was the silent fear that he *had* dreamed it keeping him from bringing it up.

Thinking of his younger brother made him smile. Mitchell was a character, as all the Benedetti men were and had been. Mitchell was aloof and charming but smart, a strong conscientious man who was now a firefighter, jumper qualified. At least he had been smart enough to avoid marrying the wrong woman. Janice was as much a sore spot with him as Rebecca was for Bram. Janice had been the closest Mitch had come to the altar. Bram should've taken his cues from his brother's reticence, but Bram married first. One more thing they had in common to draw them closer.

In command of his thoughts once more, he stood from the bed to tug the zipper closed on his suitcase to find his tickets on the bed beneath the cover. He picked up the packet, holding it in his hand, and realized with a touch of wonder that he had begun to smile. He was relaxed. It felt good to smile for nothing once in a while. His flight was early, barely after six. With time zones and an unavoidable layover, he would be arriving around eleven. It would mean a long day for him.

He wasn't entirely sure how to look at this yet. He had a guaranteed position in St. Louis, but since the divorce, if he were to be honest with himself, it hadn't felt right. Not like home. Rebecca and her constant nagging didn't help any. Even with her out of the equation, it didn't change the way he felt.

Suddenly, Selene Aiza's voice echoed in his memories. He could hear the smile in her words, her sincere expressions. He wasn't going on vacation this time, but maybe it was time to do something besides live day to day.

Finished with his packing, his bags waited by the door and his clock was set. As he fell asleep that night, he felt expectancy, a thrill that had been missing. He knew in his heart that whatever this offer was, whether he accepted or not, it was the beginning of something new for him. And for the first time in too long, he slept a peaceful, dreamless sleep.

Chapter Three

Selene steadied the slide on the electron microscope. The patient's white blood cell count was through the roof again, and she couldn't find the cause. She hated it when the little boogers hid, hated it when they made her look stupid.

There wasn't a fever, at least not as of five minutes ago, but hey, the way her morning was going, anything was possible. She wanted to snarl in open frustration but managed to keep it down to a frown as she focused the images in front of her with a delicate twist of knobs. She tugged the lab coat a little tighter around her body, restraining it from brushing against the table and jarring something.

The patient was twenty-two, a healthy male with swelling in his leg, increased pain, and a loss of circulation. The reason should have been detectable as a blood clot, but his X-rays had come back normal, and if it was there, she hadn't found it.

"Dr. Aiza, here are the results you wanted." A voice floated from over her shoulder, sliding the folder on the metal tabletop next to her.

"Thank you, Jenny." She stood erect, putting a hand to her lower back and pushing, hearing a soft *pop*. She shifted her weight and reached for the folder to look over the lab work results. She still had four more slides to review. Maybe they would give her something. She'd even settle for an infection if she could find it.

"Dr. Aiza?" a strong male voice asked, and she knew she wasn't alone anymore. Her eyes drifted closed as his scent tickled her senses, her memory.

It was as she had feared. He was the one.

"Yes?" she replied, refocusing on the patient information in her hands. She had priorities, regardless of her past rising up in front of her.

"Can I interrupt?"

"Crap!" she whispered as the cause of his high white cell count caught her eye, all but jumping off the page now that the clot had a chance to build steam. "Jenny, get this one into X-ray, then prep for surgery. I found it." The small blockage had finally grown enough to completely lodge itself. It was a good thing the patient came in as early as he had; it could have become worse and a lot more dangerous for him if he had waited.

"Right away," her colleague responded professionally from the outer hallway.

She studied the paper in her hands, hoping that if the report and the X-ray said the same thing, it was the only thing wrong with him.

"Dr. Aiza?"

Her head snapped up, whipping her hair from where it fell across her brow. She brushed it clear as a tremulous smile hit her lips. "Oh God. I'm sorry." She took in the tall man before her, his brown hair combed but soft and neat, his light brown eyes curious but sharp. "Can I help you?" To look at him again, after so long, left her slightly breathless. A raw sensation, a hum, skittered over her skin at his proximity. Drawing a slow breath, she fought to keep her realizations off her features and out of her voice. She knew who he was, had known from the beginning. The mere memory of his voice when she'd spoken to him when they'd discussed the position he had been chosen for had all but made her collapse out of her chair.

Selene would have preferred it if she'd imagined it, but the proof stood before her. This was the same man.

"Dr. Aiza, I'm Dr. Benedetti." His smile was inviting, considerate. Evidently her frazzled morning wasn't unnoticeable. *If he only knew,* she thought with a tug of her mouth.

"Dr. Benedetti," she said as she held out her hand. His shake was warm, gentle, strong, just as she had pictured him, had remembered him. The soft tingle that flowed up her arm landed in her stomach with a rush. She had no choice but to ignore it for the moment. "I'm sorry. I had a case come in early this morning that's been driving me insane. I completely forgot today was Thursday. Why don't you follow me? I have a few minutes before the patient will be ready for me to do what I need to do."

She led him down the hall of the familiar, small medical center. "What do you need to do?" he asked, a curious note in his eyes. A perfectly normal question. On most days it would have been, too.

"I need to review the slides I have remaining against this." She tapped the file in her hand. "Then if I find what I think I'm going to, I need to scrape an infection from his tibia, caused by a blood clot that I didn't see this morning that has caused another infection. Two stinking infections. No wonder I couldn't find it," she whispered to herself as she made her way into her office.

"Sounds like a day at the office for me," he joked lightly.

She lifted the corners of her mouth in understanding. "I'm sure it does. The problem with this is it's the most excitement we've seen in six months. I won't say I'm rusty, but when you don't see it every day, it isn't the first thing you think of either."

"I can understand that," he agreed with a solemn nod.

She touched the intercom on her desk as she took her chair. "Priss, can you get me two coffees, please." She lifted a finely shaped eyebrow at her guest. "Black okay?"

He nodded once.

"So how was your flight?" she began with the coffee request fulfilled.

"As normal as can be for six in the morning." She felt his eyes on her, watching as she played with the file in her hand. Why was it so hard to look him in the eye?

She swallowed down the nervous flutter that had hit when she had looked into those assessing brown eyes a few minutes before. "I'm glad. Thank you for giving us the chance. I know the board thinks very highly of you and in recommending you."

His tall length barely fit into the simple metal chair she had in front of her desk, his long legs taking up all the free space between him and the desk. Her office wasn't excessive, but she rarely had to accommodate company in the cramped space, either. He looked very professional, collected, wearing a simple suit and tie. Nothing like the first time she had seen him. She'd never forgotten his expressions of grief, disbelief, and gratitude overlaid with exhaustion, hunger, and anger all in a matter of hours of trailing him. Focusing, she tuned in to his words. She needed to be in the present to handle it all. Ruminating about the first time she'd seen him on the trails in the backwoods of her home territory would not do for this meeting.

"I was very flattered, actually." A soft frown filled his brow, his own thoughts seeming to be very intense. "To be honest, I was wondering if this opportunity hadn't come right when I needed it to." There was a wealth of meaning in those words as his gaze lightened, no longer a dark introspective hue as he relaxed.

"My only concern, Dr. Benedetti," she stressed, forcing herself to sound at ease and unruffled, "is that we might be too calm for you. Like I explained, we don't have a lot of cases like Brian to work through. We are a slow-paced, patient-attentive hospital. What we need you to consider is a position as an on-staff, on-duty doctor who could help shoulder the director responsibilities. I know it is more administration responsibility than you were expecting, but the pay difference is marginal because of the cost of living difference."

He nodded right when there was a light knock on her office door. She waved in Priss with the coffees when she peeked in. He sipped at his with a grateful thank you as she cupped hers, holding it.

"I would like to look around a bit, get a feel of things. I haven't been in the area in six years. I really enjoyed it when I was here."

She offered him a smile. "You're welcome to stay as long as you're able. The hotel room you have is comped by the committee, and they have set aside a budget for you." She made sure their candidate was treated well. Finding out it was *this* man... She was still feeling very unbalanced by his arrival. It didn't matter. He was their choice, and the hospital needed him.

His brow lifted marginally. "They really want to impress me, hmm?" He chuckled congenially as her cheeks warmed.

"Well, I gave my recommendations also," she added in a quiet tone. She'd had no idea the doctor they were researching was... She refused to add that label or finish the thought. She would have done it regardless. Bram Benedetti was the perfect fit for Bend.

A silent moment passed before the intercom broke in. "Dr. Aiza, Brian N. is ready."

Pressing the button on her side, she asked, "Is he comfortable?"

"If he were any more comfortable, he'd be riding the pink elephants instead of dreaming about them."

She groaned under her breath. "Jenny. We have company." Her guest's deep chuckle was heard from across the desk.

"Oh, I forgot," Jenny said in a sassy tone that implied that no, she hadn't.

Selene stood, facing Dr. Benedetti. "You are free to ask anything and talk to anyone all you want. I will be about an hour but after that, I should be free."

She fumbled a little bit getting out of the chair, getting her feet under her again, trying to make her way around her desk. She needed to breathe without his scent in the room, without his heat swarming all over her. The last forty minutes in close proximity had been an excruciating lesson in self-restraint. The wild reactions she'd been slammed with at the first sound of his voice, at the first lingering scent of his warmed skin, seemed to be getting worse too.

He lifted a hand to let her proceed. "Please, don't let me keep you."

She licked suddenly dry lips as her gaze collided with his. "Thank you, Dr. Benedetti. I had planned on giving you the tour myself. I'm sorry this morning has been so crazy," she said over her shoulder as she dashed to the lab. She prayed it hadn't looked like she was escaping.

Once she was inside the doorway, she fell against the wall, her heart pounding in an erratic rhythm. She sucked a deep breath. He hadn't changed in six years. Not really. He looked leaner, his smile was more controlled, not as free as it had been when she'd first seen him, but his eyes, they were the same. Those same gentle brown eyes that she had seen in the sunlight, eyes which had gloried in the warm summer sunshine.

He was who she had first suspected him to be, except six years ago she hadn't been ready. She still didn't think she was, but there was no way now to avoid him now or ignore his presence. He was the perfect candidate for the opening. If he accepted.

She shoved straight from the wall, striding to the microscope with purpose. She had a person waiting in surgery. If she found the blood clot that she was now positive would show up on the X-ray and could remove the bone infection that she was looking for, her work would be done.

Dragging in a another lungful of oxygen, she set her sights on her slide and pushed the remainder out of her thoughts.

* * * *

Bram followed her into the hallway as she rushed to the lab where he had first found her. She was not what he had expected. He had known she was young, it was in her voice, but she was also very well trained if the many degrees on her walls were any indication. He knew well enough how long earning those took.

The flicker of her hair in the fluorescent lights as she disappeared grabbed at him. Platinum blonde blended with a soft golden yellow, a remarkable fusion of light and dark. Add in incredible eyes of cloud gray and she was beyond beautiful.

Turning around, he walked the halls of the four-story hospital with a meandering gait, seeing the patterns that were and weren't familiar. The sound of footfalls, the ring of the telephone. He observed as much as he could while staying out of the way, introducing himself around but by the greetings he received, everybody knew he was there and why.

As he made an introduction or two, he realized the feeling among the staff and within those private rooms was like being home. Warm and inviting. Hospitals, in his experience, were typically cold, sterile environments because of the flow of human traffic. No chance or need to become accustomed to any one face. Yet several conversations he eavesdropped on, if only briefly, showed that here, that assumption was not the case. The smiles were genuine, and the emotions were real.

"Excuse me, Dr. Benedetti?"

He turned to the young man standing behind his shoulder; Bram's best guess was that he was in his mid-twenties. "Yes?"

"I was on my labor rounds. Would you care to join me?"

Bram couldn't hide his surprise and his gaze widened. "You handle maternity?"

He chuckled. "I know. I don't look old enough. It's all a disguise," he whispered with a wink. "I'm Dr. Davenport." He held out his hand. "Or Dr. Dave. And I'm thirty-three."

Bram laughed an easy sound, cleanly busted in thinking exactly what Dr. Dave had assumed. "You had me. I really can't see it."

"My mother's genes," he added with an unconcerned shrug. "I know you're waiting for Selene. I thought this might help pass the time."

"I'd like it. Very much." Bram slipped into step with the other doctor. "And thanks for asking."

Dr. Dave shot him an easy grin. "Hey, no problem. We all know Selene is hoping you will join. I know she's on the committee, but she is the force behind this hospital, even without the board. When Dr. Travis retired, she was the one who held it together. And for her age," he said. Bram could hear the note of awe in his respectful words. "But that's beside the point. We all thought she could do it all because she has, and Lord knows she does an excellent job at it, but this is apparently where she seems to have hit her limits."

"You make it sound like you haven't seen them," Bram remarked as they rode the elevator to the fourth floor.

Dr. Dave's laugh was short, but not unkind. "In truth, I haven't. She can go without sleep, food, or conversation for the longest that I've ever seen and still be as steady as a rock on the Fourth of July." The elevator doors opened with a nearly silent swish, and Bram followed when Dr. Dave exited.

"She sounds like quite a woman."

Dr. Davenport stopped outside a door in the maternity ward. His voice lowered in respect. "She is, and she's an incredible doctor. You will see it if you accept, but we were told to not do any arm twisting while you were visiting and I'm sure that is all I can say without breaking that order. Now then," he said as he knocked lightly, then pushed open the room door after a welcoming call. "Mrs. Ling. How are you and the baby doing? And I have a visiting doctor with me doing a tour, so please no flashing," he warned her in a joking voice. Bram was surprised when instead of being offended, the petite lady burst out laughing. She held her baby tenderly as he lifted the chart and reviewed the latest information.

"I only flashed you because I had no choice," she retorted when she had caught her breath. "I was in labor!" Her dark brown eyes glittered with open mirth as Bram felt himself relax with their easy bantering of familiar patient and doctor relations. He didn't realize until they left her room for the next check-up that he had made up his mind.

* * * *

Selene ran tired fingers under warm water, scrubbing with the antiseptic soap. There was a time the pungent smell had been so strong, it would actually make her stomach hurt. But she'd grown past it to now be no more than mildly annoying. She'd already tossed her scrubs into the bin and could hear as they finished cleaning the surgery room.

Brian should be a quick recovery. After reviewing the report and corroborating his information with the slides, her second diagnosis had been on target. He'd had a blood clot hugging the bone that had caused an infection, and it had snowballed from there. He hadn't mentioned an injury in his admittance report, but it could have been anything from a horse kick to falling on a jagged rock. He had said he'd been hiking before he came to the hospital with his leg tingling and numbing. He probably hadn't even been aware he'd hurt himself, and there were always ways to do it. She was simply thankful she had found all the components to his problems.

She finished at the sink and released the foot pedals, careful to not toss water everywhere as she dried her hands. She was making her way down the hall on the second floor when Priss spotted her.

She lifted a hand in her direction to get Selene's attention. "Dr. Aiza, your brother's on the phone."

"Okay, thanks," she acknowledged with a concealed sigh. He rarely called her at the hospital, and it usually wasn't for a good reason. "I'll get it in my office."

She closed the door and sat, taking a long relaxing stretch before hitting the blinking button on her phone.

"Morgan? It's me. What's up?" She pushed the now cold cup of coffee from that morning as far away from her as possible. She'd dump it when she got up. Next year sounded possible.

"Hey, thought I'd let you know, I've been out and the traps are back." No, not good news at all.

That was not what she wanted to hear. "Damn it!" she ranted quietly. She rested her head in a hand, massaging her forehead with stiff fingers. "I thought we got rid of him last year."

"I'd hoped we had too," he said, the sound of resignation in his voice. "But I guess he didn't take the hint, and we're not done. The traps are better. Either that or it's someone else."

"Is that what you think?" She closed her eyes, propping her head on her fingers, feeling the tired she'd been fighting crawl all over her body.

"Not hardly." Morgan grunted. "They're set the same, and they still stink."

She wrinkled her nose at the remembered smell. "Whoever thought that smell made good bait needs to be shot anyway."

She heard the grin in his voice, imagined the flash of his teeth. "I feel the same way."

Her head snapped up at the inquiring knock on her door. When it cracked open, she waved Bram in. "Look, Morgan. I need to go. I'll see you tonight and we can talk about it. Maybe we'll find him in person this year."

"I can't wait," he replied with an anticipatory growl in his voice. She knew exactly how he felt. "Love you, sis."

"Love you too, brother." She settled the phone in its hook as Bram took the chair in front of her. She had smelled him on the other side of the door. Now that his scent was familiar again, she'd know where he was within a mile, easily.

She rubbed her eyes briefly trying to decide what to say, how to start. There was a lot riding on Bram Benedetti's acceptance of the position. She'd been pushing herself to fill the demand for over a year. She hoped she wasn't being selfish praying for this relief. She'd keep up the pace if there was no other option, but she needed a rest. She needed to run free. She'd had to stay close and hadn't had any real time to enjoy the woods like she had with Morgan and Brooke in the past. She couldn't deny the need to clear her head either, to figure out how Bram was supposed to fit into her life, now that he was clearly in it. If he stayed.

"Problems?" His query was concerned, crashing her thoughts into scattered shards.

"Not too much." He lifted an eyebrow at her vague attempt. "Nothing that bears on today, anyway." She shifted her body, leaning forward to rest on braced elbows. Back to business. "Have you had a chance to explore?"

"I have." He steepled his fingers in front of him as he regarded her in turn, a steely curiosity in his brown gaze. "However, I am curious to know why everyone already knows who I am and why I am here. No one seemed put out by that."

She felt the heat rising on her cheeks as she straightened her spine. "Dr. Benedetti, I asked for good behavior, but if anyone had done less, I would have known. Your addition is important to this hospital. Regardless of if you think that is presumptuous or not, you are needed here." Her mouth thinned into a line, fighting her weariness and the defensive nature it seemed to be bringing to the forefront.

"How long has it been since you've had a day off?"

Her eyes rounded at the question. "Excuse me?"

"How long? And don't try to cover it up. I think I already know the answer." He regarded her with a stare that seemed to burn right through her.

"It isn't relevant, doctor. I assure you, we're all perfectly—"

"And I'm aware of that. Please, answer, Selene." His words slid over her, a wave of energy that she couldn't ignore. Her throat went dry hearing her name on his lips. God, how did he do that? If only his voice could knock her senseless? When Roman had told her it hit and it hit hard, he hadn't been kidding.

She hid the quiver in her own voice as much as possible knowing he'd take it as insecurity when it was the furthest from the truth. "Eight months."

He was stunned into silence for several seconds. However, his words when he found them were explosive. "Good God! You've been running this hospital and staff for eight months straight?"

She nodded once, sharply, not letting his reaction sting her. She knew she was capable. He didn't, not yet. "It's been necessary."

He sagged into his chair. "But surely there are others in the community—"

She raised a hand to stop him. "Dr. Benedetti—"

"Bram, please." He cut her off, calmer after his outburst.

"Bram," she relented. "I've already been through the community and neighboring systems twice. It was by my hand that you're even here." His brow rose at the implication of that statement. She felt her resolve stiffen as she laid it on the line for him. "What I am offering is not a big city practice, but an entire hospital."

"Who are you?" he asked, bewildered.

"I am Selene Aiza, director, specialist, doctor, and nurse. I work any and all shifts, can perform any surgery within my knowledge and probably a few that I did by the seat of my pants, but I have found I have limits. I wasn't kidding when I said I had done an exhaustive search looking for the right person to come here. I have looked for over two years."

"Why did you choose me?" His expression was as stunned as her previous words had left him, but now he sounded equally perplexed.

"You had the credentials, experience, and the bedside manner that we want. We did research your background extensively to make this offer." She saw as his lips curled at the loose use of *we*. She supposed he knew the truth about that now, as well. "But even beyond that, you had something that I was looking for."

"What?"

She gave in to the urge and rubbed tired eyes. "The ability to adapt. Your reaction to situational circumstances in your history is what drew my eye, professionally, over a year ago. I need someone who can walk in here tomorrow and know what is going on and be able to handle the pressures that come with it. We aren't big, like I said. I'm sure you've seen that, but the communities do rely on us. I won't let them down. I need to know the person chosen to aid and support this hospital won't either."

He nodded once, slowly, as if considering her reasoning. "I can understand that."

She stood, weary beyond measure at the day's events, and it was still early afternoon. "I don't expect an answer today," she informed him. "Or even by this weekend. And I will not use tactics to try to sway you. I want a sincere, honest answer, yea or nay."

He held the door open for her when she rounded her desk to exit the office. She faced him in the hall, aware that all her hopes for his acceptance were in her gaze. She'd never been a good poker player. Morgan took her to the cleaners regularly.

She felt something gentle wash over her with the way his gaze lingered on her face. "If I gave you an answer today and told you it was sincere, would that work?"

She shook her head firmly. "I couldn't possibly ask you to make that decision in less than four hours. This is too big for casual consideration. You would have to move, make notice, find a place to live. No, I couldn't ask that of anyone."

"No wonder everyone speaks so highly of you," he said under his breath.

When she turned to walk to the nurse's station, he fell into step at her side. "I'll tell you this," he told her, standing next to her when they reached it and she grabbed the next file. "I can honestly tell you that I accept. I made the decision two hours ago, if that will alleviate any concerns. In ten days' time, you are to plan at least four days off from on-duty time."

"Dr. Benedetti..." His gaze silenced her when she looked up at him.

His mouth was firm when he told her, "No. I need this as much as you do. I didn't know how much until I got here."

Her vision swept the length of the hall, torn between wanting to jump at the opportunity of having him join the hospital, what having him there would ultimately mean for their continuation and stability, and between what his presence would mean for her. It was too hard to even debate at the moment. Her own needs would have to be ignored completely.

When her silence stretched out, he continued. "I will see to what I can while I'm here. I have until late Monday before I am due in St. Louis. And I will take the first step by forwarding my resignation after we've stopped for lunch."

She couldn't fight the relief as it welled up inside of her. She blinked away the pressure behind her eyes. She was more tired than she thought if this was messing her up so easily.

His voice was kind when he turned her by the shoulder, facing him.

"You're not in this alone anymore. In fact, you might have given me exactly my reason to keep going."

She trembled catching it before it overtook her, then dropped her chin a little. "Sorry," she mumbled. "I had my hopes, but even I know better than to put too much weight into certain ones."

"Somehow, I think I know exactly what you mean," he told her before he gave her a smile. The one she remembered. The real one.

He stepped away and offered a hand. "Dr. Aiza. It will be a pleasure to work with you."

Her hand settled in his, warmth covering her skin. A roaring rushed against her ears as her heart sped up. She plastered on a smile to hide her physical reaction. "I look forward to it, Dr. Benedetti."

Bram studied her, seeing the growing fatigue in her cloud-gray eyes, the overdone smile. The apparent need of a break was so out in the open, he wondered how anyone else hadn't noticed, or had and couldn't do something about it.

"Now, how about that lunch? I know you haven't eaten since I've been here." She stilled with the exact grace of a startled doe.

"I really couldn't." She turned away from him, and he let her hand fall away. Facing the counter to sign a patient release form, she hid her expression from him. It was something he had already discovered: she had a very expressive face. A beautiful, expressive face.

"When was the last time you ate?" he asked, remembering what Dr. Davenport had mentioned.

She waved a slim, dismissive hand. "I eat when I can. I always eat when I'm at home," she informed him. She faced him again, a disarming smile on her lips. "I'll be off in a few more hours anyway. Please don't worry over it. I'm used to it."

"Well, I know that's one of the things that will change when I get here. You shouldn't be used to not eating."

Her quiet laughter brushed off his concerns, but her smile lightened as she explained, "Please, really. I know, I know. I hear it from my brother constantly. I keep snacks in the lounge, under order from the big bad brother."

Her assessing look went from the top of his head and traveled the length of his body. Her voice was gentle and lower, a private statement between them when she said, "I knew I was right about you. I hope I was right about everything."

There was nothing sexual in her tone or in her gaze, a blunt honesty that showed how much she had put on the line to have him there. It made him respect her further for being a careful and dedicated individual.

"All right, then. If you're sure I couldn't tempt you?" he offered one more time. She had turned as he spoke and he was almost sure that she had blushed a rosy pink hue at his words, but the curtain of hair hid her from his view. She shook her head in answer. "Okay. I'll be in touch before I leave and before I return."

"Thank you again for considering." This time there was no mistaking the lowered huskiness of her voice, even though she didn't look up to speak to him. "And thank you from all of us for accepting."

If he hadn't recognized and caught the impulse, he would have kissed her. Right there in the middle of the floor with nurses passing and patients' doorways standing open. Her whole body spoke of vulnerability, an attitude that he wouldn't have believed a part of the strong-willed woman he'd begun to know. He cleared his throat as he forced another few inches between them. "You're very welcome, but I think I'm the one who should be thankful."

"Good, then both of us can be grateful," she said, a flipped rise on her lips that flashed along with the humor in her eyes before she nodded once more and left him to administer and check on patients. His gaze followed her as she disappeared around the corner, unable to not watch.

"Doctor. Doctor? Dr. Benedetti?" He shook himself, focusing on the young brunette who manned the counter. "Are you all right? You look a little flushed."

He laughed ruefully at himself. "Yes, thanks. I'm fine." He swiveled his attention down the hall. "I've never met anyone like her," he admitted.

"Dr. Aiza is a real gem. Everyone really does love her. No one was putting on a show, if it crossed your mind. We all adore her, even when she has to be firm."

He turned to lean on his elbow, his attention split between the nurse behind the counter and woman who had vanished down the hall. "How long has she been working here? It sounds like she's very well known."

"She's been here since she started her training."

By the closed off look that followed, that was all the young lady was saying. He patted the counter with a palm. "Oh well, thank you."

He turned on his heel and left the hospital behind him as he set the next course for his future.

* * * *

Monday, Bram contacted the hospital to let Selene know that he was returning to St. Louis, but he wanted to talk to her personally. For three days, as he'd made arrangements for moving his life, he hadn't been able to forget her. He was disappointed to be told that she wasn't due in until second shift, and he couldn't explain why it was so imperative he talk to her that day, right then, to see her before he left. He was going to be working with her, every day, for a very long time.

Bram made his way down the highway after getting directions to her place from the hospital, telling himself the purpose was strictly professional. Doctor to doctor. He wasn't interested in women at the moment anyway. He placed that foremost in his thoughts as he started to hit the forks that led to her home.

He found the cabin in the clearing and knew it was the right place. It looked like her. A home. A place of serenity and beauty. The wood of the cabin was bleached, though the natural red hue still shone through. There were wide windows that opened to the front porch with a large overhang. The landscaping was natural except for a few well-placed rocks, or maybe they were meant to look that way, he mused as he turned off the vehicle engine.

He sat and waited for a greeting of the canine type. When none appeared, he slid from his rental and closed the door. He couldn't resist the urge to breathe, and that he did with zestful abandon. The scent, the warmth. It brought peace.

As he started to walk for the front door to knock, he saw it. The animal looked like a large dog in the shadow of the house, watching him intently. As it stepped out into a band of sunlight, a careful paw forward at a time, he blindly reached for the hood of his car with a shaking hand.

The wolf from his vision!

He gaped in awe as they stared at one another for a few brief seconds, then with a flash of its tail, it turned to disappear behind the cabin. As his mind started working again, he straightened. No, it couldn't have been. He'd dreamed of that wolf. Wolves did not live out here, and certainly not this close to people. Although after the drive he'd made, he knew he was farther out than he had anticipated.

His head snapped up when the door suddenly opened to find Selene standing on the porch, staring at him with cool curiosity. He pushed off the car, refusing to admit how seeing the wolf had shaken him.

"Sorry to bother you, but I wanted to catch you before I left," he began.

"How did you find me?" Her gaze was closed now, not entirely welcoming.

He offered a rueful smile. "I asked and the personnel department gave me directions, but it took some work. I am sorry for intruding." He looked around, feeling like an invading army among the peacefulness of her little slice of heaven. "I can see why you like your privacy."

Her expression lightened a little. "I do. You took me by surprise. The only other people who know where I live are family."

"Isn't that dangerous? A woman by herself out here?"

She leaned against the closed front door, crossing her arms in front of her. "I'm not entirely alone."

"I saw the dog. It's beautiful, but not exactly a good defense. It ran."

"She knew you weren't an enemy."

His lips twisted at her blunt assessment, really not wanting to argue over the dog's behavior. "I should have called, but after Thursday I wanted to make sure you understood I had accepted." He caught a slight flicker, maybe relief, pass over her features before she straightened in front of the door.

"I'm glad of that." She inched forward to stop at the edge of the top step. "Can I ask how you got them to give you directions?"

He knew he flushed at her frank question. "I told them I had already received documents that would transfer my insurability and I wanted to get them to you."

Her lips lifted at the ploy, an arched eyebrow emphasizing it. "And did you?"

He knew he'd been caught. Lying had never been one of his more skilled traits. "You're too smart for your own good." Did he look guilty as he said that? Most likely.

Forgiving laughter followed her as she came the rest of the way off the porch to stand with him. His gaze flickered over her white shirt and bleached denim shorts to land on bare feet.

"It's all right. All I ask is that you don't give out the secret."

"I was warned you like your privacy."

"That isn't a secret," she answered glibly. "So when is your flight?"

"In a few hours. They're not happy with me at home." He let his shoulders sag a little.

"Ah, therein lies the reason. You don't want to face their wrath."

"I know I shouldn't be surprised, but are you always this astute?" He was getting too comfortable with her, her smile, her laugh, but he still couldn't make himself leave. He found himself grinning too much.

"It's an unfortunate character trait that runs in my family. We're damnably smart," she said in playful jest.

"Yes, I can see that. Well, I'm glad I at least got to say goodbye before I had to leave." He reached into his jeans pocket and withdrew a note paper folded in half. "Here are my contact numbers. If you need anything from me, please call. I have a timeline, but nothing ever goes to plan."

She stared at the numbers held in her hand. "No, no they don't," she replied in a distracted tone. When she lifted her head, his breath hitched at the way the sunlight glinted in her gray eyes, a turbulent blending of shades drawing him in.

He'd fought the impulse once, but now there was no one, no nurses, no audience, no reason not to as he started to lean down craving a single sip, a taste. Her lips had parted, an alluring shape that called to him. He'd been wanting to for days, he realized, even as he swore he wasn't interested in women; he was intrigued by this one.

The shrill cry of the phone from inside her cabin jolted them apart. She skipped a hurried step, alarm and something more in her expression. She turned without a word and ran for the house. The phone was answered two rings later. He straightened, shocked to find his breathing ragged and bordering on a full arousal.

It was time he left.

Chapter Four

Selene stared out her window long after Bram had driven off. If it hadn't been for Morgan's call, she would be in deep water right at the moment because no matter how much everything about Bram said he was the one, she wasn't ready.

Her eyes closed as the picture of him standing in the sunlight came to her. Tall, virile, and dominant but so very tender. She had sensed the tenderness in him on more than one occasion. His general caring of a person's welfare, a concern to make the world right. It was in his work, in the way he handled people. The way he handled her.

She shook her head, letting her forehead touch the glass pane of the window. Now that he was here and would be staying, she knew her resolve was going to be tested. The secret of her home was only the tip of the iceberg.

Six years ago, it had been folly to do what she'd done, but her curiosity had won over caution, and he had needed help by the last day she'd trailed him. Now, she felt ill-prepared, slightly anxious, and incredibly nervous about the direction things were taking, how quickly they were moving, and now he knew where she lived. When no other soul outside of her family knew of her little cabin, he did. Someone at the hospital had given him directions. That could have been from the faculty file, for all she knew. His arrival in her territory was only a first sign.

The second had been the near miss of his kiss. She still gripped the slip of paper with his phone numbers, unwilling or unable to release that link yet. She didn't know what had possessed him to try to kiss her, and she didn't want to analyze why she would have let him.

Evidently, six years had not been enough preparation for her to accept fate's calling. She laid the slightly crumpled paper on the table by the phone and went to change for her shift at the hospital.

* * * *

Three weeks later Bram had successfully listed his home, which wasn't heartbreaking in the least. His resignation hadn't been taken as well, however. They had pleaded with him, offering a better salary, more benefits, anything to tempt him to stay, but they couldn't offer the one thing that Bend could. A sense of peace that came from doing what he was meant to do. He was done with St. Louis. Done with the demands, the criticism, the around-the-clock assholes who ran his life like a puppet on strings. He was burned out on what they were offering.

He had contacted Selene earlier in the week to keep her up to date on his plans since it was taking longer than he'd originally hoped. She'd sounded surprised at first, maybe justifiably fearing that his plans had changed because of the near incident Monday at her cabin when he'd left and that he wouldn't be returning because of it, but he quickly destroyed that notion.

He had rented an apartment the weekend he was there and had already sent the movers ahead with his things. He was flying out in the morning. He was ready for the challenges ahead, passing hours in a hotel room, an excited anticipation flowing through him.

Ready to start over. Ready to find what he had been missing all those years in St. Louis. Just ready. There was only one last thing to do.

Rebecca.

Lifting the phone, feeling a heavy dread, he did what had to be done. He frowned as her voice sliced across the phone line at his news. "You can't mean it, Bram! You can't!" she cried into his ear. He yanked the phone away, waiting for a pause.

"I do, and I have. I'm flying out in the morning, and I will be on staff in less than four days." She should be thankful he had opted to call her at all. He lifted his eyes to the ceiling. Her thinking, however, never would have come to that conclusion.

"Where?" The demand was unmistakable in her voice, in that one word.

He shook his head, knowing she expected him to relent, to bend. *Not this time. Never again.* "Out west."

He heard as she ground her teeth over the phone. "Why won't you tell me?"

"Because we both need the distance," he replied.

"But Bram..."

He sighed. "I told you ages ago it was over. Hell, I told you that when the divorce was final. It's over. You haven't wanted to hear me. You haven't wanted to believe me."

"I love you." She sobbed harder.

His mouth tightened, disgusted with her antics. "Rebecca, I don't love you. Let it, let us, go," he entreated her.

He heard the sound of her expected tears and couldn't even dredge up remorse any longer. "All right, Bram. I'll miss you."

Seconds later, he said goodbye. There was nothing left to say. He slid the phone into the cradle, standing from the corner chair of his room to look out one last time at the city he had called home his whole life.

As he stared out the window, he thought about the day he was preparing for. He was heading for a new job, a new home, a new life, and as his thoughts moved and merged, the weight of the phone call, the chill of his own failures at whatever level, no longer felt so heavy on his shoulders.

His mother and Mitchell had both taken the news in stride, his mother probably more aware than his brother at the restless, caged feeling he had felt burdened with the last few years. He had explained the change better to them than he would ever think of for Rebecca, with the exception that his mother had exacted one promise. He had to keep in touch. They were still a family.

His lips rose as he remembered the discussion with them. His mother had asked covertly about Selene when he'd mentioned her by name, but his attitude had been impersonal, as was appropriate. They would be working together. He'd used the same description she herself had used, keeping his own observations silent.

Like the way her hair had shined in the sunlight, or the way cloud-soft eyes seemed to change shades with her thoughts. The way he had been tempted twice to kiss her, when he knew it was the last thing he should have even been considering.

He did tell them about her work ethic, how protective she was of her staff, how much she and her staff cherished their patients. She was a remarkable woman who had endured a lot, eight months' worth, and now, in less than a week, he would be working with her.

Moving from the window, he slipped off his shoes to stretch out on the bed. He padded his hands beneath his head. She was remarkable in so many ways. No one on staff had uttered one bad word about her. In fact, the majority had praised her and her ability. Honest, fair, levelheaded, and no one seemed to even notice how beautiful she was. But he had.

He had noticed it as he'd neared her in the lab with her head bowed over a medical file, cursing about an infection. His lips curled at the corner at the memory, his mind recreating the slope of her shoulder, the arch of her neck.

His drifting eyes snapped open. Was he attracted to her? Was it possible? He'd all but sworn off women after Rebecca. He was going to be working with Selene now, even though for all the definitions there were, he was pretty sure she was going to be running the show.

He shook his head in adamant denial of his feelings. There wasn't any way. All things considered, a physical attraction was not only impossible, it was a bad idea. He shook his head once more in agreement with his decisions as he relaxed again.

* * * *

Four days later, he made his way to the nurse's station carrying a box, having already spent the morning with personnel. "Good morning. Is Dr. Aiza in yet?" he asked the dark brunette who had manned the counter during his previous visit.

The young lady stood and formally introduced herself, stretching out her hand. "Priss by name, and yes, she never leaves, Dr. Benedetti."

He chuckled at the affectionate accusation. "I'm here to see that she can."

Priss sighed with a grateful smile. "Good. We're all very glad you decided to join us, doctor. She needs a break."

"Is she in her office?" he asked, already turning in that direction.

"No, she's in surgery, but she should be available in about thirty minutes."

He shook his head. "Is she a superhero or something?"

"The *or something* qualifies," Priss replied, grinning easily, walking from around her desk. "I do know which office she was going to offer you, though. If you'll follow me," she suggested.

"Sure."

A few minutes later he had dropped off the box of notable frames and his name board. It was a regular office, several feet larger than Selene's, he noticed, but knowing how much time he would really be spending in there, space wasn't of great importance.

He meandered out to the station desk. "Do I have a roster yet?"

"You do, but Dr. Aiza would like to go over it with you to cover any questions you may have. You're welcome to make yourself at home," Priss assured him.

"Would she mind if I took it and waited in her office?"

"I doubt it." He accepted the clipboard, nodding to her inquiry of if he remembered where her office was.

"I do," he answered, already absorbed in the patient reports under his nose.

He sat for a while reading and becoming familiar with his patients. It didn't take long; there were only six patients today. What a difference from the workload he usually carried.

After he read the reports, he let his gaze wander around her office. She kept it simple and very neat. There were no loose files on her desk, no lost papers waiting for a home. He was surprised at how organized she was considering the responsibility she alone had carried. He rose to read her degrees on the wall when he spotted numerous frames, curiosity getting the better of him.

He swallowed in disbelief. "How did she do all of this? General medicine, a midwife certificate, and surgery specialty." There was also a business minor. She couldn't have done this for her age. She wasn't that old. He was positive she was much younger than him. Well, maybe not much younger. He was only thirty-two, but it did explain how she had held the hospital together after the previous director had retired. She knew what she was doing, but it didn't really answer how she had studied in multiple fields. "She must have started as a child."

"Close," her amused voice said from behind him. Her eyes were laughing at him even though she didn't do it out loud when he turned to face her. "You should close the door if you plan on talking to yourself. Save yourself explanations and claims of insanity later," she playfully advised.

He pointed to the degrees. "How?" His confusion showed in the one word.

He let her move behind her desk, taking her chair with simple grace before sitting in the one he'd claimed. "You were close. I was advanced for my age. I graduated high school at fifteen with honors and entered Berkeley with recommendations. I overlapped my courses, at least as much as they would let me. I knew I wanted to come here, and the sooner the better. I knew what I wanted to do when I was in the womb. At least that's what my mother has always said."

"Amazing," he told her with a note of awe. "I busted my rump for eons, I think."

"And look where it got you," she said, a teasing glimmer in her gaze. "A cushy co-directorship, specialist position that most would puke their liver for."

He laughed kindly. "True." He lifted the clipboard from the edge of her desk where he had set it after reading it over. "Is this my roster for today?"

"Yes, and I can almost guarantee it won't get any worse than that unless either myself or Dr. Dave is gone. Then you have both lists, but Dr. Dave is very reliable. There is also Dr. Lin and Dr. Calvin at our disposal. They have private offices. But even with that," she mentioned, pointing at his roster board, "your day here will be lighter than your average day in St. Louis."

"I could get used to this," he said, and he couldn't stop the smile that filled him. He was relaxed, calm in a way that had been missing. He did have a good spot now.

"I'm glad you see it that way. I know I'm ready for the extra help."

He straightened immediately. "I'm sure you are. When are you leaving?"

"I'm sorry?" She gave him a confused frown.

"You are to take time and rest. Doctor's orders," he insisted as he crossed his ankles and waited.

She waved a fluttering hand, letting it drift to her desk. "I'm not taking any time off. I'll be happy if I get to sleep for more than four hours and take an occasional run," she told him in a dismissive tone. "I'll be fine."

He was confident she knew what she needed but withheld his opinion for the moment.

* * * *

With Bram on call for the next four nights, Selene
and Morgan slipped through the forest searching for
the traps that he had found a few weeks earlier. They
found six, too many considering the volume of land
they covered. The pair either damaged them beyond
usefulness or threw them high into the trees where
they couldn't harm an animal or unsuspecting person.
There was little doubt it was the same poacher they
thought they had deterred the previous summer when
the first traps had been found. With the final one
mangled beyond usefulness, the siblings loped to
Selene's cabin, a night's work done.

Once they stood in the clearing of her cabin and
were dressed, she asked him if he knew who the
poacher was.

Morgan shook his black-haired head. They were
as different as night and day. "I don't, but I think I'm
getting closer. I found his trail three days ago, but I
had to let it go and haven't had a chance to try again."
They walked side by side to reach her front door, both
lost in worrisome thoughts that a poacher was hunting
their lands. It was clear he was after a wolf by the bait
scent, but there weren't any wild ones that far west of
Yellowstone or the Rockies. That made the problem a
lot larger. Frighteningly, a lot more personal, as well.

She nodded, her thoughts subdued as they made
their way inside to close the door behind them. "Well,
now that Bram is here, I can help more."

Morgan tossed himself with insolent care onto her
couch. "Do you still think he's the one?" he asked. She
walked into the kitchen but heard his apprehensive
question.

Returning from the kitchen with a beer for him
and tea for herself, she curled up at the end near his
feet. "Morgan, do you remember what Roman said

about when he found Delilah? About knowing?" she asked, her voice as pensive as her thoughts were scrambled.

He sipped on his beer as he contemplated the ramifications of what she was suggesting, his eyes closed as he appeared to remember his brother's reactions to finding his mate. He groaned a sympathetic sound. "Yeah, I do."

Her finger traced the rim of her cup as she spoke. "I knew when I saw him six years ago, but I was too young and I was still finishing some of my studies." She shook her head, wanting to argue against fate. "I didn't *know* it was Bram until he walked into the lab that Thursday morning."

"So what are you going to do?"

She smiled weakly at the brotherly concern she heard. She let her head fall forward, her hair covering her face in a platinum wave as the enormity of what that question was hit her. "I don't know. I just don't know."

There was a shared silence between them for a few brief minutes. "I want to meet him," he told her.

She lifted her chin with a snap, her gaze wide. "Morgan..." She was already shaking her head.

He glared at her, his protective side glowing in his dark gray eyes. "Selene, you are the youngest. I'm the oldest."

"So?" she ground out.

"I want to meet him," he repeated, an imperialistic demand in the dark depths that stared at her.

The contest of wills went on for several minutes until she grudgingly relented. She understood why, but she didn't have to like it.

"Fine," she said under her breath in a snarl. "I'll see what I can do."

"That's all I can ask, now isn't it?"

She didn't grace him with an answer.

When Morgan left for his home deep in the Cascades, she walked outside, feeling the night air surround her. She'd already been out once tonight, but that had been to serve a purpose. She longed for the feel of the breeze, the call of the night owl as she sped by.

She stripped on the porch, assured of her privacy. She closed her eyes, listening to the earth, the wind, the stars as they enveloped her. She found the beat of her heart where it tripped against her ears. She was a creature of the night and welcomed its pull, the nocturnal call as old as time itself as she cocked her head to listen.

She felt the warmth spread through her body, urging it, commanding it. She scented the air, the aromas intensified by her long, delicate snout as her lupine shape overrode her humanity. She found the family of squirrels locked away high from the forest floor, asleep and unaware. She could smell the rain miles away as it drifted near the coast.

She lowered her head and sniffed the ground, but it was the same as it had always been. It was her home. Her den.

She shot off the porch at a sprint into the tree line and felt truly free. Humanly concerns were not of this world, the one she was a part of, in possession of. Not the need to find a mate, to fulfill a crying urge that had awakened six years ago on the trails of the Sisters. Not the concern that she had work in the morning. None of it mattered.

For a few bliss-filled minutes, she was wild. She was wolf.

When she hit the clearing again, barely an hour had passed but she stopped at the edge to cautiously scent the air and the ground to ensure her den had not been invaded. Until Bram's unannounced arrival a month before, the only male scents she had ever allowed had been her brothers. She prayed that wouldn't be changing any time soon.

She padded up to the porch and called on the powers of the goddess she was named for, the powers of the moon and the night, to reclaim her human form. It took hardly a minute to go from four feet to two, having long ago mastered the archaic nuances of her shape-shifter ability.

She gathered her clothes, reentering her still quiet home. She was restless as she showered and prepared for bed, but it was an achy restlessness, a pervasive feeling awakened when she had found Bram lost and emotionally hurting on the trails. Six years of preparation simply were not enough.

That night as she slept, her dreams wandered around Bram. His caring, earth-colored eyes, his laughing smile. As the images developed, the wolf appeared, seeming to overlap between herself and then Bram until there was only a single image. A melding of Bram and herself with a shadow of the wolf between them.

She woke in the morning, an uneasy feeling in her stomach and a shy fluttering near her heart. It was a lot to consider and even harder to believe. Just because it was meant to be didn't mean it would happen.

Dreams were only images, and in that, she was thankful. Dreams could not inflict pain. She rose, remaining adamant that she was not ready. It was her only safety net.

Chapter Five

Over the next month, Bram's schedule was full, yet not hectic or demanding to the point of draining. It didn't bring the feeling of oppressive burnout that he had needed to escape. He slept well at night. Rebecca didn't call at all hours needing answers from him to questions he wasn't going to discuss. And he learned to appreciate Selene's dedication and experience.

She wasn't as young as he had first thought. She was thirty-one, which in his opinion intensified his respect for her role as hospital director. The hospital ran like clockwork. Everyone was family.

She was also a very reclusive woman, as he'd found out. The only thing he had been able to discern from the staff that worked with him was that she wasn't married. Other than that, either they weren't talking or there really wasn't anything about Selene to talk about, which he found highly unlikely.

There was some quality, something almost different about her, drawing him to her. He'd witnessed her calm a distraught woman with nothing more than a glance and a word. A firm hand clasp and a tender smile were her drugs of choice. She was the most precise surgeon he'd ever run across, and her ability to work her teams like a drill sergeant amazed him.

He had also discovered that she worked outside of the hospital doing house calls and aiding senior citizens who were incapable of seeing a doctor by themselves. Who made house calls in today's world, anyway? Dr. Aiza did.

While doing one of those house calls, she'd invited him to join her, to introduce him to a few of her patients in case he ever needed to do backup for her, and he witnessed something he knew he couldn't explain.

The lady they were to see had her son visiting and he had brought his dog, and as he recalled, it was a Rottweiler, a large one. Selene, calm and composed as always, walked to the gate and made a sound, a vibration he could barely hear, but the dog stopped growling and barking like it wanted to eat them both for lunch. She opened the gate and waited for the dog to approach them. Bram could only stare in wonder as the dog rolled over on its side and let her run a hand over its chest when she crouched down by its side.

With a final tummy scratch, she stood and walked right up to the front door. "Don't worry; he won't harm us, now or ever. He knows we're friends," she had said, making her way with Bram following, one eye on her and one on the dog, but it was as she had said. When they left, the dog bumped her with his head looking for a farewell pat. And those were only a few of the qualities that he had found intriguing about the woman he worked with.

"You're smiling again," Selene said as they reviewed the latest cases in her office.

Bram straightened in his chair, unaware he had let his thoughts be so easily viewable. "Is that bad?" He cocked an eyebrow at her, trying to hide his embarrassment of being caught not paying attention.

"Depends." She pressed a finger next to her place, marking it.

She lifted her head, and he was struck again by her beauty. When she smiled, there was something almost familiar in it. He dismissed the notion as whimsical.

"Is it bad to smile?" he asked in a bantering tone.

"We're discussing a cancer patient. I don't think they'd appreciate it," she said, his eye being drawn to a twitch at the corner of her mouth.

His smile deepened. "I would have to agree with you there." He sat up in his chair as he realized he was feeling something akin to attraction again. He started talking, wanting to ignore the realization that it might be. "Actually, I was thinking of how well of a job you've done keeping everything smooth and how much I have enjoyed this. I was right when we met. I did need this."

Her smile was beautiful, and it nearly toppled him from his chair. "I'm really glad you feel that way," she said. "I knew you were the right person, and I'm glad you're happy. More than that, really." He noticed a wary, cautious light flash across her eyes. There was a hesitation as she looked at him, then past him.

"Is something the matter?" he asked.

She cleared her throat once. "Well, I have been asked to introduce you to someone."

He felt a chill settle over him. His tone was cold as he said, "I'm sorry, but I'm not interested."

Her mouth dropped open as she shot him an appalled look. "No! It isn't like that. I wouldn't do that to an enemy, much less a friend. I don't set people up," she informed him with a slightly affronted inflection. "I was asked to introduce you to a major contributor of the hospital."

"Oh." Bram shifted his weight and offered an apologetic smile, wondering if his embarrassed assumption was as obvious as it felt. "Sorry. I guess I jumped to a conclusion there."

"Pretty sure of your looks there, doctor?" she teased.

He fought the spasm of laughter, stifling it down to a chuckle. "I deserved that," he said a moment later. "I would be glad to meet whomever."

She nodded once. "I better warn you, though." He waved a hand when she paused, playing with the corner of the file on her desk instead of looking up. "He's my brother."

"You're kidding?" He was surprised to see her flush, a pretty pink that suffused her cheeks for a brief moment. She focused beyond his shoulder again.

"No, I'm afraid not. He's got his finger in a lot of pies and when I started here, he became one of the largest contributors we have."

"You're here because of him?" The short-lived glare she shot him disavowed that idea. She didn't need anyone to pave her roads.

He heard a short strangled sound. "Hardly. He's helping because I told him to, but he likes to play feudal lord every now and then and make demands. Meeting you is one of them," she replied, her voice controlled and pleasant again.

"Understandable." He watched as she visibly relaxed with his agreement. He swallowed as her gaze flickered over him. He had been right. Ignoring it, but right. He did want to kiss her. The smile she graced him with only enforced it.

"Thank you. Would this Saturday be all right?"

"I would be happy to. Tell me when and where." His gaze strayed to her mouth, and he felt a rush of blood below the waist.

"The cabin at seven ought to do."

He was having a hard time paying attention, but he made himself do it. "Should I bring anything?" he offered.

She shook her head, platinum hair flowing in a short, sassy wave around her shoulders as she rose from her desk, closing the file they had been discussing. He lifted himself from the chair to follow her, careful to keep his lab whites closed.

He caught her words as they entered the hall. "You don't have to. I'll make sure they know where to find us if they need us."

"Sounds great." His gaze fell to hers, and he felt it again. That *need* becoming insistent. He watched as her eyes darkened, a thought behind the wall of the woman. His body's reaction was immediate and powerful. This was worse than a mere attraction. He wanted her. Badly.

She licked her lips. The sweeping movement of her tongue leaving a glistening dampness to the light pink of her bottom lip dragged the air in his lungs to a standstill.

Her voice was breathy. That could've also been the thunder of blood as it raced through his body making her sound that way, too. He grabbed onto his self-control with a steel strength.

"I better go check on this one." She twitched the file she held in a death grip in her fingers.

He forced his legs to take a step in the other direction. "Sure, sure. I, uh, have a few to do myself." She nodded once, adding a tilt of her head, then she turned on a heel to leave him standing in the hallway.

He marched to his office and closed his door, a hard shudder traveling from his shoulders downward when he released the pent-up breath he'd been holding.

* * * *

Selene stood over the oven in her kitchen, checking the roast, then timing the bread. Morgan was in the living room watching TV. Bram would be there any minute; she'd heard the thrum of an engine a few minutes before as he crossed the creek that ran south of the cabin and the clearing.

She slid her hands over her jeans repeatedly, then yanked down on the hem of her pale blue sweater even though it hadn't moved. She lifted the lid off the steamed vegetables and wrinkled her nose. Those weren't for her. The bread was toasting well. She check the time again and reached for something else to keep her hands busy.

"Relax," Morgan called from the living room.

"Sorry," she said, forcing herself to calm down. "I can't help it. I've never had a male guest inside."

"I know," he answered, understanding in her brother's voice, which didn't really help her all that much. Her head snapped up as the sounds from outdoors reached her. Bram had arrived.

Morgan walked to the open kitchen door frame where he stopped, inspecting her. "He doesn't know anything, right?"

She shook her head with a rushed shake. "Of course not."

"Then there's nothing to worry about. We'll talk, eat, and he'll leave. End of evening."

Their heads turned in unison to the knock on the door. "I'll get that," Morgan offered as he moved toward the door. She gave him a weak smile. She was too nervous to think, much less try to make small talk.

She heard her brother introduce himself, then lead Bram into the living room. Why couldn't they have done this in town? At a restaurant? Why at her house? She fought down the surge of panic threatening to overwhelm her. She tightened her shoulders, stiffening her spine. No big deal. Morgan was there and the evening would have an end. It *would* end.

She drew a deep, calming breath and was unprepared for the effect Bram's scent had on her senses. It hit her with a force of a fall hurricane, nearly knocking her to the floor. Selene grabbed for the counter with white-tipped fingers as he filled her entire being, overloading her thoughts.

She'd been fighting this powerful surge ever since he'd arrived. For over a month she'd tried to ignore what he was, *who* he was. Tonight, he was in her home, her den. The heat swelled, blossomed across her body to burst within her with longing. She turned, entranced, toward the sound of his voice, her low-heeled boots clicking on the wood floor.

She needed to see him, a peek of what he looked like when he wasn't a doctor. Her memory was strong, but it was six years old, and no matter how she fought it, she could no longer deny or fight the yearning his presence brought out of her.

He was undeniably handsome talking with Morgan, both men sitting in the matching chairs fronting the fireplace on the east wall. The large windows on the rear wall let in the last of the evening sunlight, and it shined directly on Bram's brown hair. His gaze was focused, glinting in the sunlight like running water. His pressed shirt and slacks accented his lean, tall frame. She felt the floor shift.

"Selene!" Morgan called sharply.

Her vision cleared to find them both staring at her. Bram's brown eyes filled with worry, Morgan's with understanding but issuing a warning.

She clasped her elbows, forcing her body to obey. "Dinner is almost done," she said. "Excuse me. I need some fresh air." And before Morgan or Bram could question her, she fled out the front door.

She thought she heard Morgan say she had been feeling a little tired today as she hurried out, but any excuse he gave would be flimsy. She knew the real reason behind her discomfort, and it was the furthest from exhaustion that she could think of.

She inhaled draughts of surrounding air, finding the scent of the forest, the trees, the ptarmigan nested off to her right, the aromatic earth–each scent until she found her balance.

This was only dinner, after all. She could make it through one evening.

With that thought in mind, she turned to go inside, thankful to see Morgan had brought Bram into a conversation.

* * * *

Bram studied Selene out of the corner of his eye as she nodded and smiled at them, gaining his attention when she spoke. "Sorry about that. I got a little lightheaded."

"No problem," Morgan said. "You ready to eat?" he directed to Bram.

"Sure. I made sure to at least bring an appetite," he said with a grin, glad to see Selene smile at the memory of their conversation.

"I'm glad. I cooked enough," she remarked as they made themselves comfortable at the table. Selene brought out a roast that looked like it could have rivaled his mother's, it looked so good. She had made a vegetable medley and bread. He murmured his appreciation as he took a long inhalation.

"Glad you approve," she said with an easy grin. "I don't cook that often. I have wine if you would like some," she offered as she gave herself a large goblet of water.

"That would be great."

Morgan sliced the roast as Bram watched Selene secretively from under his lashes. "So, Dr. Benedetti, how are you finding Bend?"

He quickly shifted in his chair to focus his attention on Morgan. "Bram is fine, and I like it a lot. I was out here when I was younger, and I've always wanted to return." Bram filled his plate the same as his hosts and waited.

Selene lifted her glass up. "To friends, food, and life," she toasted.

Morgan emulated her with his wine, so Bram followed suit. "That's refreshing. Family tradition?" he asked as he tasted the wine. He was surprised at how well it flowed over his tongue. She knew a good wine as well.

Selene's light laugh turned his gaze to her. "You have no idea. Dad can go on forever when he has company."

Morgan groaned with agreement. "Yes, he can. I remember the one time he had that congressman come out, forgive me I don't remember his name, but the politician had come out trying to persuade Dad's political affiliation. Only Dad outmaneuvered him by being the long-winded one."

"That was a dinner party I could have missed," Selene groused. "I had to wear that atrocious gown. God, where did Mom find it!" she wailed.

"I don't know, but you could have been pretty if you hadn't snarled all evening," Morgan teased her with a brotherly chuckle.

"Selene doesn't snarl. She demurely demands," Bram offered lightly as he sank his teeth into the roast and savored the beef cut. "This is wonderful."

Morgan and Selene joined in his laughter. "She can be very demanding," Morgan agreed. "And even if she doesn't aspire to chefdom, she can cook quite well."

"I would have to agree there." He offered Selene a real smile and was rewarded by heightened color on her cheeks. He liked watching the rosy hue that warmed her skin when she did blush.

"Do you have any brothers or sisters?" Selene inquired, nibbling in slow bites.

"I do. Mitchell is three years younger than me and a firefighter in St. Louis. He recently finished his jump training and with his pilot's license, he can be called anywhere in the country. He's a remarkable man nowadays."

"Unlike, say, when you were young?" Morgan quipped with a wave of his fork and a look that said he understood.

"That would be right. What about you two? Who's older?"

Morgan started the rundown. "Well, I'm the eldest son, firstborn, then came Roman six minutes later, then Brooke three minutes later, and Selene was last, twelve minutes after Brooke. She's taken her sweet time about everything since," Morgan teased her with a brotherly stare.

"Quads? Seriously?" Bram stared between them, then remembered to shut his mouth when he feared he may be gaping.

"Afraid so," she replied. "None of us look alike, except that Morgan and I have Mom's gray eyes. Roman got the brawn; he's six-five, by the way. Morgan got the looks, Brooke has an ingrained affinity for nature, and I have the smarts with a dash of compassion. That's how I knew I wanted to be a doctor. I live every day to make someone better and healthy."

"Amazing. I've never met a twin, much less a set. Not counting the ones in the hospital nursery," Bram said as he pushed his plate forward. He noticed that he wasn't the only one who'd been hungry. Two more nearly empty plates were pushed forward. "So, what do you do for the hospital, Morgan? Selene had said that you are a contributor."

"I am, but the whole family is. I work with the National Forestry Service between here and the Pacific Northwest corner, but I only live about five miles from here, so we're close. The others are a little more scattered."

"Speaking of scattered, have you heard from Roman about Delilah?" she asked her brother.

"No, not yet, but she should be due any time now." Morgan turned to Bram. "Roman married a little over a year ago and their first child is due. We're all waiting to see who wins the bet."

"Bet?"

"Sure, boy or girl, day, time. The usual," Morgan explained.

Bram laughed lightly. "What family doesn't do those things is what I'd like to know."

Selene rose from her spot, saying, "Go on out to the living room. I'll clean this up and join you in a minute." She shooed them off with her hands.

"Okay, don't push," Morgan whined. "I'm full."

"Yeah, sure you are. You and I both know you could eat the whole thing by yourself," she admonished him. He gave her an answering grin that bordered on wolfish as he made his way out of the kitchen.

Bram began to follow his host but noticed Selene gripping the counter, concerned when she seemed to pale and flush simultaneously. "Selene, are you all right?" he asked her, worry for her filling him.

She nodded with a sharp movement. "I'll be fine in a minute."

Bram lifted a hand to her shoulder, wanting to turn her around to look into her face, needing to see that she was all right, but his concern grew when she shuddered under his touch. "Selene?"

She started shaking under his palm. He twisted her around to face him, lifting her chin to search her features. When her eyes opened, they were the color of soot, a charcoal gray unlike any he had ever seen.

It was at that moment he knew she wasn't ill, with her chest rising and falling with ragged gasps. Her breath was a hot brand against the hand holding her chin. "Bram," she whispered, a plea of confusion.

"Selene," he said, lingering as he stood before her. His head tilted to hers before he realized he couldn't stop himself. She gasped as he made contact. A seductive heat filled him, made him hungry in a way he had never imagined when his mouth covered hers.

He stopped in a shocked rush, dropping his hands as if he'd burned himself. Maybe he had. "Oh, God! I'm sorry." He was nearly panting. He shook from the power of the kiss, of her lips, as they'd melted against him.

Her eyes flashed at him, and she snaked a hand to wrap around his head. "I'm not," she whispered, pulling him down.

She controlled the kiss, the heat, the hunger. It was all Selene's doing as his hands settled at her waist, holding himself steady. His heart beat with a trip-hammer intensity against his ribcage as she urged him on. She moaned softly when he aligned himself against her body, the shape of her form filling him the same way her kiss was flooding his senses.

She shuddered in his hold when he flicked out his tongue, touching the edge of her soft mouth. Her reaction shot through him like a liquid fire. He became consumed by her kiss, her touch. He became lost in her as he took the kiss over from her, feeding off her.

She moaned again, deeper, a vibration that heated his blood to boiling.

He forced himself to stop, to lift his head. Or else he would make love to her.

The realization was as chilling as an ice-cold shower. He was not going to get tied up with another woman. "I'm sorry," he told her, clawing to regain his composure. "I didn't mean for that to happen."

Her eyes focused once more as she released him, a sharp guilt filling them instead. "I understand. I shouldn't have—"

He lifted a finger to silence her, pressing against her still-rosy lips. "Shh. That was my fault, and even if I shouldn't have, I don't regret it."

Her gaze was unsure, confused. "But I—"

He shook his head, not letting her continue. "I don't regret it," he told her, his voice lowering to a gravelly sound, unable to stop himself from reliving the sweetest moments of her kiss. She shivered before him. "I'm going to tell Morgan thank you, then I'm going to leave." He slid a quick step away, forcing a space between them. "Thank you for having me and for letting me meet your brother. But if I stay..." He couldn't finish the thought. "I have to leave," he repeated.

And even though his entire body was screaming for him to make love to her, to hold her, to please her, he made himself turn away. It was the hardest thing he had ever done.

Chapter Six

Selene stayed at the counter bracing herself, listening when several minutes later, she heard the front door close and released a shaky, pent-up breath. Her breathing was still erratic with the scent of him filling her, the memory of his kiss heating her lips the same way his hands had to her skin.

She'd been powerless, filled with him, with wanting him. Needing him.

Her head drifted forward weakly as the push of blood against her ears eased. She had to acknowledge the truth now. There was no way to avoid it. Her gaze followed the tracking of his car's headlights as they faded slowly into the darkness.

"Selene?" Morgan stood behind her, well aware that what she had experienced was obvious, written all over her face.

"How did Roman do it?" she asked, torn with indecision, with a hunger she didn't understand and a need that she couldn't control.

"I don't know. It's different for each one of us, every generation."

Her head sagged forward again. "Why does it have to be so much harder for us?" she agonized.

He turned her into his arms, holding her as he had when they were still children. "I can tell you this: he's as much off-kilter as you are."

"So if we both fight it, nothing will happen, right?" She looked up at him with a hopeful, unsure stare.

"I'm not saying that. Go with your feelings. Trust in what you know," he advised, brushing her hair with tender fingertips. "I need to get home. I have a long assignment coming up near the Washington state line." He kissed the top of her head. "You will be fine." He looked into her eyes, so similar to his, filled with love and tenderness for her. "I've always thought that between you and Brooke, you were the sensible one. Maybe in this instance, a little imprudence is what you need."

"You're not suggesting..." She gasped on a shocked breath.

"No, of course not, but be open to things. You've known this day was coming for six years. You can't hide your head in the sand forever."

She laughed shakily at his analogy, curling into his embrace. "That's an ostrich."

He kissed her forehead and left her to her thoughts.

* * * *

Bram felt strange the entire drive to the highway. Overheated, overwhelmed, needy. He snarled loudly as he moved his Explorer off the highway to a scenic roadside park. He got out, slamming the door.

What had he done? He marched with long strides beside the vehicle, trying to fight the sleeping beast her kiss had awakened. He stuffed clenched hands into his pockets, frustrated that he'd allowed his impulses to come so close to the surface. He could vividly remember every touch, every caress, every breath that had passed between them. It brought him right to a full aching arousal.

He stopped pacing, leaning instead against the side of his vehicle while he heaved in deep gulps of air.

He stared up into the night sky, naming constellations without conscious effort. His fingers gradually relaxed from their digging positions into his palms as his mind's focus changed.

He could think logically about this. It had only been a kiss. Granted, one he'd wanted since that first meeting more than a month ago, but it was only a kiss. An aberration. He'd lost his perspective. He worked with her. He admired her. He respected her.

He wanted her. And he suspected she wanted him too.

Was she attracted to him? Except for that brief glimpse in the hall earlier in the week and again tonight when the signs had been right on the surface, he could have probably let himself believe otherwise, but even he couldn't ignore the spark that had ignited when he'd held her in his arms.

She was so much…everything. Compassion, beauty, brilliance, intelligence. A complexity of a feminine puzzle that even upon their first meeting he'd felt drawn to.

No! He snarled it openly into the night. No, it wasn't possible. She was just another woman. He'd had enough of women. Rebecca had taken his soul and warped it, twisted his wants around her finger until he no longer had any idea of what direction was up. He'd barely escaped with his skin, and he knew it. Misery or not, his only saving grace had been her realizing that he would have divorced her with or without her approval.

One would have taken longer and would have been far more painful for the both of them, and Rebecca was an all-image woman. She was wise enough to let him go with very little dirty fighting, even if he did have to let her keep the house to be free.

He crossed his arms as he bowed his head, his thoughts tumbling around him like a macabre shadow of his own life. That meant the only way to keep this from getting out of hand was to prove it wasn't already a disaster. They had to face each other on a near-daily basis. There wasn't any way he was going to let this get out of hand.

Opening the door with a determined yank, he slid behind the wheel to return to the cabin. He would apologize. He would take the blame. He had started it. He would vow it wouldn't happen again because there was no way it could repeat itself. And a kiss was a *only* kiss.

He stopped next to her Grand Cherokee, waiting for the dog that hadn't shown up since the first visit he'd made. He wondered as he got out where it stayed since it didn't stay close to the house. But it wasn't his concern. He only wanted to–

He jerked on a heel as a shot rang out, echoing in the distance. It wasn't close, yet the report was still loud enough to echo through the trees with a fading sound. Who would be using a firearm at nine at night? He spun completely around in a circle, searching for any sign of where it had come from. When after several minutes it didn't repeat, he moved with cautious steps to her door. He frowned when there was no answer to his knock. He looked through a window. The only light he could see was in the rear of the house. The cabin itself wasn't large, and the illumination could have been from a bedroom or a hallway.

He knocked again but thought better of calling her name. He really didn't want to see the dog face-to-face if it decided he wasn't friendly.

There was a possibility that she had gone somewhere with Morgan as he strode to his car. He was reaching for his car door when he heard grunts, and the wild sound of crashing branches to his right. As his eyes sought the shadows, a shape rose from the ground within the trees, a fluid motion of impossibility.

Yet, even as his mind couldn't absorb what it had seen, it instantly recognized the blonde who now stood there, and his mouth went dry.

"Selene!"

Her head whipped around, her eyes wide with fear and pain before she collapsed to the ground, completely naked.

He was beside her instantly, uncaring of the trees in his way. Lifting her, he ignored her naked state. When he turned into the moonlight, he found the reason for her unconsciousness. She'd been shot above the swell of her right breast. Blood coated her limp hand where she had tried to stop the flow.

Oblivious to anything beyond seeing her safely inside, he was relieved to find the door unlocked, striding to the rear of the house. The illumination had been from her bedroom. He tossed the blankets with a rough yank, scattering the small pile of clothing that had lain there.

"Selene? Can you hear me?" he asked as his skills took over. He found her pulse, still as strong as her breathing, only slightly erratic from pain.

She moaned softly as he lifted a sheet to cover her. "I'm going to get my bag," he informed her as he jogged from the room. When he returned, she still hadn't moved. "You need to go to the hospital, Selene. This is too deep," he said as he examined the wound closely.

Her hand lifted from the sheet to find his arm. Her eyes were glazed and bright with pain when they opened and found his. "No. Hospital," she said, biting the words out through clenched teeth. "Remove. Here."

"Selene!" he cried, a tortured groan of indecision.

"Please. I trust you." Those were the last words she said as unconsciousness stole over her again.

He gritted his teeth at her stubborn nature. He did notice the blood had slowed but the only way to do anything at all about the wound was to remove the bullet, which would restart any bleeding.

"Damn it!" He gave her one quick glare, then moved to the restroom to wash his hands. As clean as he could be, he pulled out tweezers and a capped scalpel, suture thread, and a pre-threaded needle.

In less than five minutes he'd lifted the bullet enough to grasp it and, with a final tug, pulled it free with a squelching sound. He dropped it on the bed next to her as he put pressure on the wound with a towel he'd filched from the bathroom. Once the bleeding slowed, he took a good look at the wound. It was still a good inch to inch and a half deep.

"You need to have this looked at," he mumbled as he started closing the wound with the threaded needle. Now that the worst was over, he started ranting at her, his quietly growled reprimands the only sound in the room aside from their combined breathing.

"What were you doing in the woods, stark raving naked anyway? Were you trying to find trouble? Morgan told me you've had poacher problems. Are you trying to get killed? Crazy woman."

He snipped the thread as he made his last knotted stitch. "And how are you going to do anything now? You can't lift, you can't go to work." He shot her a look. "I get it now. This was your way to take your vacation and not look less than superhuman. You're forced to take it now."

He rose from his crouched position next to her bed, gathering his instruments and the errant bullet. He rinsed everything in hot water, setting them on a towel to dry. He'd sanitize them the next day when he restocked his travel bag.

As he washed his hands, his gaze fell on the bullet that now sat on the rim of the sink. He was slammed by a blunt shock as he realized he had removed a .22 caliber bullet from her shoulder, one that had been deep enough to kill if it had hit something vital. "Good grief, how close were you?" he whispered.

His head swiveled over his shoulder, seeing her resting figure on the bed while the bullet weighed on his mind.

He checked for a temperature, but she felt cool to his touch. He grimaced when he remembered he'd washed his hands. Not the best for temperature testing.

"Bram?"

He tugged the chair that sat along the wall up to the bed. Her eyes were still closed, pale lashes resting against curved cheeks.

"I'm right here," he said. "You need to have that looked at. What were you doing?" he asked, feeling extremely cross at the predicament she had put him–them–into.

Her hand lifted to find his arm, resting without pressure. "Please, don't be mad. I'm sorry I scared you," she said as she swallowed.

"Hold that thought." He jumped from his spot and, finding a cup in the kitchen, brought her water.

She drank with a grateful sigh. "Thank you." Her eyes opened to his penetrating stare, a soft, silvery gray that reminded him of something, a fleeting memory. He pushed it away as his concern for her rose with a more adamant strength.

"Look, I don't know what you were doing or why, but I took a bullet out of your shoulder. Even though you're awake when you probably shouldn't be, I can't leave you like this. You need to at least be looked at."

"I was," she said with a sincere smile. "By the best doctor we have."

"Selene!" he cried with exasperation.

"Bram, I'll be fine." She closed her eyes tiredly, even though her color seemed to be returning. "I'll rest and in no time, I'll be good as new. Nothing to it," she said with unconcerned grace. "I am sorry you had to do it, to see me like that."

"Naked? Well, it wasn't what I was expecting when I came back."

"Why did you come back?" she asked. Her hand remained on his arm. He placed a hand over hers, suddenly unsure how to answer that.

"You should be resting, not talking."

"Fine. You talk, I'll rest. Why did you come?"

He was surprised at how sharp her gaze was when he finally lifted his to look at her instead of where his hand was. There wasn't even a shadow of pain any longer.

"Don't you hurt?" he prodded.

"I can push it out of my mind." She squeezed his arm. "Now, answer the question. Please."

How could he answer it? In a matter of an hour so much had changed, or not at all. There was only one way to find out.

"Selene," he began as he searched for the right way to put it. "The kiss? I don't know." He wanted to stand, to pace, to leave so she couldn't see the truth, or hear it. "I swore off women after I divorced Rebecca. I didn't mean for it to happen."

"I know you didn't," she offered. His arm had begun to tingle where her hand rested. Her eyes were closed again as she listened, resting as ordered. "But I wanted it, too. I didn't realize how much until…"

"Until I started it," he finished for her. "It won't happen again." He thought a frown flitted over her face, but if it had, she'd been too quick to hide it from him. He patted her hand. "Look, you rest. I'll tell them you've taken a day or two off."

"I'll be fine," she assured him, but she sounded distracted. Probably from the pain.

He sat with her for some time, carefully monitoring her for a fever, until she fell asleep, her hand trustingly captured under his.

He watched her for more than two hours, waiting for the first signs of a fever. When she continued to rest peacefully, he knew he needed to get home and get some sleep himself. He'd be pulling double duty at the hospital with her in the condition she was in.

It wasn't until he was halfway home to his apartment in town that he realized she'd never explained why she had been out, running wild and naked, or how she'd been shot.

* * * *

Selene woke in bed where Bram had left her the night before, and the first thing that hit her was a gnawing hunger. She wasn't surprised. Blood loss required iron and protein. Before she did anything about it, though, she took an inventory of her parts. She poked a finger at her shoulder and winced at the tender pain that lanced through her. The worst of it was healing over already. The swollen flesh had mostly returned to normal, and the redness would be gone soon as well.

She lifted herself from the bed, slipping on her robe as she padded to the kitchen. She took out some beef tips and, warming a skillet, browned them enough to take the chill from the meat. She ate them like popcorn, popping them and munching one after another as she made her way to her room. Sinking to the edge of the bed, she lifted the phone at her bedside to call in and see how things were holding together with her unexpected absence. She was startled in the process of making that call by a knock on her front door.

She glanced at the clock. It was after ten, and she didn't even have to guess at who was standing outside on the porch. She may not have heard him, but she knew who it was. She left her emptied plate on the nightstand, wiping her hands on the towel that had covered her shoulder for most of the night. Blood was blood. It would eventually come out, she mused as she made her way to open the door.

She was hit anew with the overwhelming male scent that was Bram and trembled weakly when it swung open. She felt herself weave a fraction of a step, but it was enough for him to notice.

His words were gruff when he lifted her from her feet and carried her to bed. "I knew you were full of baloney. You shouldn't have moved." He laid her down, slipping the robe over her. "I could have let myself in," he reprimanded her as he pulled the sheets and blanket up.

He was very aware she was still naked as a jaybird under her robe. The knowledge was in the way he avoided making eye contact until she'd been covered. So he wasn't as unaffected as he'd played last night. Her heart tripped a little over that.

"I'm fine. I was about to call in and see if they needed me," she told him.

"It's quiet on the front. You, on the other hand, need to rest." He pulled the chair close again as he opened his bag. "Let's check you out." She held out her wrist and let him check her pulse, which had sped up erratically once he touched her again.

She knew the bond was going to get stronger. Her blood had been on his hands. It was becoming stronger every second. She watched as his gaze widened when he finished timing her count. "How are you still standing?" he wondered out loud.

She almost laughed, wanting to tell Bram it was him and not her wound that was making her react, but he wouldn't believe her. Not yet. But that was about to change. Drastically.

"Shoulder, please," he said as he stared at her, a clinical tilt to his chin. All business, all professional.

She bit her lip, suddenly shy. Not because he'd seen her, but because he was about to see more of the truth.

"Come on, Selene. I'm a doctor, and so are you. Anatomy is that." Was that a hitch in his voice? She tried to look at him out of the corner of her eye, but he was focused on the collar of her robe, no lower, and definitely not where she could make eye contact.

"Okay, but you asked for it," she muttered. She sat up, leaning against the pillows behind her for balance. She shrugged her shoulder and let the robe gape open, baring her upper body to the swell of her breast.

"What the hell?" His face blanched as he stared at the shoulder, all ready for the exam, to have his hand float slowly to the bed.

"I told you I'd be fine," she reminded him.

"Obviously," he said, completely distracted by what he was looking at. "Where did it go?"

"It's still there, very tender in fact," she explained.

"A wound that deep does not heal overnight. Not even in a week." His mouth was slightly open as he lifted to meet gazes. Shocked was only the beginning.

He leaned away as he continued to stare. She rewrapped her robe, pulling the collar up as she waited for the first questions. When he remained silent, she began to feel uncomfortable.

"Bram, if you want to ask, do it. Otherwise, I'd like to dress and brush my teeth. I've only been up about an hour."

"At least you slept well."

"Yes, thank you for that," she said as she clasped her fingers in front of her, her head bowed as she waited.

He half rose, then plunked down onto the chair. "If I let you dress, will you tell me anyway?"

She knew what he meant. She could feel it like an arc of electricity between them. A spark, and all they would have to do is touch again to send it into a full, raging bonfire.

"I will tell you what I can." It would have to be a compromise. This was happening too fast between them, too fast for her. It was the most she could offer.

He nodded once and, gathering his bag and exiting with a quick step, closed the door to give her privacy behind him.

She released a soft sigh. Why did finding a mate have to be so difficult? Why couldn't she fall in love and that be it? Why did what she was have to be a factor? And why did love have to be so damn elusive?

She was done and dressed in less than ten minutes, padding out to the living room on bare feet. She carried the plate in a hand, but her steps slowed when she realized what he was staring at.

No, that was too much. *It was way too soon,* she thought putting the plate on the kitchen table.

"You have beautiful paintings," he said.

"I'm surprised you didn't see them last night. You and Morgan were right underneath them," she said as she stepped into the room. She wrapped her arms around her waist, fear and trepidation keeping her from saying more.

"I've seen this one," he whispered. He pointed at a beautiful oil painting of a pale white wolf, head raised in a full-throated cry of freedom with a nebulous moon hanging like a hole in the sky. "I thought I was imagining it. A vision. I was lost, and she kept reappearing. I don't know."

He stopped talking, looking at her with a rueful grin. "I've never spoken of it to anyone. I didn't know if it was real, and I didn't want to know if it wasn't."

"Do you remember anything about her?" she asked, unable to hide the hesitant hitch in her voice, stopping a step or two away from him.

"Only that it had these incredible, piercing gray eyes. The coat in the painting is exact," he said with admiration. "Whoever did the painting is extraordinary."

"My father did them," she said. He still stared in inspired wonder at the painting that hung to the right of the fireplace.

"Your father is very talented."

"I'm sure he'd be glad to hear it from someone other than his adoring family," she said with quiet humor in her voice.

"Is this wolf still in the area? I've always wondered what she was doing this far west," he said, distracted and probably drawn into his memories.

"Yes, she is." She took a fortifying breath. "That's part of what caused last night's problems."

He spun to face her, his attention rapt, which she had intended. "I was out last night tracking the poacher, but he backtracked on me and shot at me. I wasn't quick enough to avoid it."

"You mean the poacher that is stalking the woods? He's looking for that beautiful creature?" His face was frozen between shock and outrage.

Oh yeah, she had all of his attention now.

"I told you I'd explain what I could. I owed you that much for being here when I needed you," she told him honestly. She swept her foot back and forth as she gathered her thoughts. "Morgan and I have been tracking him since last year. We thought we'd gotten rid of him. We've destroyed thousands of dollars in traps, I know that. I guess in his meanderings through the Pacific Rim, he's caught sight of the wolves that do live here and since they're not banded or tracked, he thinks they're fair game."

"How many wolves are there? Surely the preservation society is aware?"

She shook her head. "I doubt it. They are very reclusive. I know they don't care for humans."

He spun, pointing at the white one. "But what about that one? She was not a mirage."

Selene's voice wavered again. "No, she wasn't."

He looked at her closely. "You know of her, don't you?"

"In a manner of speaking, yes."

There was an unescapable expression in his gaze as he stared at her. "And you've seen them, all of them? How many are there?"

"I've seen them all. Out here, there are three." She could feel him trying to connect the dots. It had to be his realization. She wouldn't do more than point the way. It would be better if it didn't happen today. Too much of anything was not a good thing.

He shook his head as he turned and paced a few steps. "It doesn't make any sense. You were out after dark." His head snapped up. She watched intently as his eyes went unfocused at the memory. "And you were naked. What happened? How could you have done anything at night?"

She minced a pace away, not going any further and not offering any more. "I can't explain that, not now.

I wouldn't know how even if I wanted to," she said barely above a whisper.

His face froze. "Can you explain the healed shoulder?"

"It's an ability everyone in my family shares." She shrugged, offering an indifferent stance, but she couldn't meet his gaze. It wasn't exactly a lie, but it certainly wasn't near the truth, either. "Morgan's the one who has actually been doing the tracking. I had a dumb luck run-in with him."

She twitched again when he stopped pacing in front of her. If he touched her... When she moved, though, his face jerked, like he'd been slapped. Her throat tightened. She was beginning to feel desperate. He was too close. She was too aware. "You should probably try to forget it. You should go to the hospital. I'll be in later, second or third shift, to compensate."

"Just forget it?" He growled as his jaw tightened. "Just forget that I saw you collapse naked in the grass? That I dug a bullet out of your shoulder? That not even twelve hours later you're more than seventy percent healed?" His hands captured her shoulders, and she gasped as his heated grip singed her. "How can I possibly forget? I haven't been able to forget one thing about you!"

She knew what he was going to do. She couldn't have stopped him if she'd wanted to. She didn't even try.

His lips landed on hers with possessive force. His promise to not repeat last night was completely obliterated as his desire enveloped her, igniting the spark that flared between them to sunburst levels of intensity.

She didn't have the strength to fight the way her body wanted to respond, demanded to. The ache biding its time under the surface flared to life with his touch as his mouth captured hers and commanded her.

She molded herself against him, feeling him along her body. His hands were firm as he anchored her, his arms sliding around her body to keep her there. She whimpered when he used his tongue against her, demanding access.

She felt alive, completely absorbed in him, in his touch. He shuddered beneath her fingertips where she stroked his lean frame, regretting the hard-fought signs of control when he softened the kiss. His breathing was as ragged as hers when he lifted his head, but only so far as to look at her.

"Selene." His voice wound down her spine with a sensuous caress. She shivered lightly from the shock. Her eyes drifted opened, searching, but unknowing for what.

"Your eyes," he whispered. He spoke as if from far away. "You have these incredible gray eyes. They remind me…" His words were slowing, his expression becoming withdrawn. Lost in memories.

"They remind you of what?" she prompted gently.

His smile was easy, but the shadow in his gaze was her answer. *Denial*. It was for the best.

"It doesn't matter." His hands loosened and he stepped away from her. "It's time I left. That is, unless you need something."

Only you. "No, I'm fine. I should be capable by this afternoon." He started to reach for his bag. "You didn't tell anyone about last night, did you?"

He paused briefly. "No. It didn't seem prudent under the circumstances." He faced her again, the calm and professional doctor once more. "But if anyone should ask, you can always say we split the shift or something for personal business."

"Thank you. I'll be in a little later." She reached for the door as he walked out, waiting until his car was out of sight to close it.

Chapter Seven

A few days later, she was walking the halls as if nothing had happened at all. No one that he'd heard had even raised a question to the sudden unexplained switch of shift hours. She was relaxed and smiling with everyone.

Well, almost everyone. There was a definite tension between them, and it had been his fault for it. He should have left well enough alone. But he admitted it would have been impossible.

The way she made him feel when he was with her... He felt protective, for one, and regardless of what had been the catalyst, if she was anywhere nearby, he would know. It was almost as if he could feel her, a touch on his skin, a whisper in his ear, and he would know.

The memory of her kiss was still there, too. The soft warmth of her, the burning heat, the hungry desire that was Selene. He'd found himself walking around for hours with a half arousal because he couldn't shake the memory.

This was all new to him. He'd never experienced what he felt when he was with Selene, never desired like he did for her. The picture of her smile, her hair, her eyes. There was something about her eyes, a memory, but every time he tried to place the connection, he lost the thread of connection.

He was distracted in those same thoughts when the phone on Priss' desk rang, breaking into his introspective reverie.

"Of course, Chief. We can send two. Yes, repeat it. Yes, I have one here." He straightened at the intensity in her voice, matching her drawn expression. "On their way." She hung up and paged Selene.

"Dr. Benedetti, that was Chief Swarenson. He needs backup for a multi-car accident. The EMTs are understaffed this month," she said, standing in agitation.

"I'm here," Selene said, gasping as she jogged up to the counter.

Priss handed her the details. "He's out on the interstate, but they had a rollover in the ravine and two are missing. They need hands and doctors."

"I'll go," he said without thinking.

"We'll take the Jeep," she said. "Page Dr. Dave. I'll make sure one of us comes back with an ambulance to help." She rushed without a backward glance to the double doors, Bram close on her heels.

He prepared himself as she drove with sharp, quick precision to the location of the accident. It had been a while since he'd been paged out for any kind of on-site emergency. It was a different kind of adrenaline rush, a different environment. A lot more could go wrong.

"Jesus," she whispered. "Six, seven cars. What the hell were they doing?"

"That's not counting the rollover."

They spotted Chief Swarenson and Gabriel Markson, his deputy, as they slid to a gravel-spitting stop on the shoulder while Chief Swarenson directed the paramedics that they did have and the three volunteer firemen to aid with the low-grade injuries.

"Thank you for coming so quickly," Chief Swarenson said over the loud popping of a door being wrenched off its hinges. "Two of our guys are on vacation, and of course a third's wife went into labor this morning."

"No problem. Where's the rollover?" Bram asked as he looked over the metal carnage.

Chief Swarenson pointed to a destroyed safety rail. "They hit and went over by the nose. One of our guys is down there now, but he says a passenger is missing. Get down there and see what's going on." The chief shot them both a grateful look as they spun to slide down the damaged embankment.

"Jeffrey, it's Selene. What's the status?" she said as she skidded to a stop at his side.

The paramedic nodded as he cradled the driver's broken arm, wrapping a splint. "Drugs. All over the damn car." He tossed an angry chin over his patient. "They're stoned out of their minds. I wouldn't be surprised if they caused this," he said with a tight jaw and jerked head, meaning the wreck behind them.

"Where's the other one?" Bram asked.

Jeffrey looked over the undercarriage of the upside-down vehicle. "He ran off into the woods. I doubt he made it too far. Probably passed out. There's still a kid inside."

"I'll see if I can find him. Where are the cops?" he asked as he rose.

"They're on their way." Jeffrey finished the splint as Selene began to crawl inside the vehicle for the child.

He clutched his bag, keeping it secure as he searched the tree line. He spotted a sapling broken in half and started his search. He wasn't an expert tracker, but even a blind man could follow the trail this guy had left behind. There were broken branches, and overturned limbs and debris, revealing recessed craters of decay.

Bram was glad he'd left such a good trail because the missing person hadn't passed out nearby. It took over ten minutes to find the splayed body of a thirty-something male facedown in the leaves.

"Okay, big guy, let's have a look at you," he said as he started to turn him over.

"Get your hands off my brother!" The hair on the back of his neck rose at the ominous threat from the voice behind him.

He slowly raised his hands, making his actions obvious. "I'm a doctor. I'm here to help."

"I know what you are, but no man is going to touch my brother. Never again."

Bram swallowed. Whoever was behind him was so drugged up, his words were slurring.

"Look, I can't help him if I can't touch him."

"And I have a gun. So back off and leave him alone!" The command was panicked. He started to stand with calculated slowness. When his captor didn't protest, he turned around and faced the biggest nightmare of his life.

A young man with a laceration down the side of his face and eyes so dilated his irises were completely hidden held a .44 pointed square enough to make a hole the size of New York in his chest.

"I can help him," Bram said evenly. "He's been hurt." Bram had seen a sizable gash across the other man's head before he'd been stopped.

The younger man sneered, waving the gun, keeping Bram immobile. "Ronny is not having another man touch him." Bram watched as tears tracked down his pale and pinched face. "He's not gay! I don't care what he says. He can't be gay! He's my brother!" he shouted as his face scrunched tight with amplified agony.

"I'm not going to hurt him. And believe me, I'm not gay," he offered. "I'm a doctor. I can—" He froze in shocked disbelief as a streak of pale white shot from the bushes, a low growl deep in its chest as the animal lunged for the arm holding the gun. Bram dropped to the ground as a shot and a sharp cry of fear echoed through the trees.

Bram shook his head, alleviating the ringing in his ears. Within seconds, he heard the moaning cries of the youth a few feet away. He was curled up, cradling his arm and sobbing into the dirt. "Ronny!" he shrieked endlessly as Bram lifted himself cautiously to his feet.

He spotted the gun and kicked it farther away. He searched in all directions for a sign of the attacking animal but saw nothing, not even a flicker of fur. He glanced at the gunman's held arm and couldn't find a single mark of broken skin. Shaking his head, he opened his bag and withdrew a syringe for a sedative shot. His patient didn't even flinch as he plunged it into his arm. A minute later he was breathing evenly.

"Bram!" His heart leaped when he heard her searching shout.

"Selene! Be careful. There's an animal—"

"I saw it. It's gone." She cut him off in a matter-of-fact voice.

He looked up from his position over the injured man. Her hair was tousled, and her lab coat was gone. His eyes widened as she turned to check on the sedated body and he saw her shirt. It was buttoned wrong, and the last pale pink button was missing.

"What happened to your shirt?"

She glanced down. "Snagged it," she said after a thick second. She avoided his gaze for several heartbeats. His mind was brought to the present as the body at his feet moaned.

"Easy there. We need to get you guys to the hospital," he soothed. His fingers were sure as he worked over the man's body.

"Concussion likely, a dislocated shoulder," he said as he searched.

"Selene, Bram! You guys okay? We heard a gunshot," Jeffrey shouted as he barreled through the trees, followed by others carrying litters.

"Yeah," Bram replied as he pointed in the gun's direction. "That one's sedated, this one's out." He turned to Selene. "What happened to the child?"

"She didn't make it. She wasn't wearing a belt or in a booster." Her voice cracked and he wanted to reach out, to soothe, but with four others as witnesses, the most he could do was nod. Her expression said it all. Sometimes being a doctor sucked. He helped strap the injured men down, then followed as the procession started toward the roadside. The sound of sirens and metal being moved wafted down the embankment into the trees. It sounded like more crews had reached the accident site.

He looked over his shoulder and found Selene standing with her head bowed, heaving in deep breaths. Walking up to her, he stopped in front of her. "You all right?"

She nodded stiffly. "You could have been shot. I wasn't thinking."

Suddenly concerned for her, he folded her into his arms. "Shh. I'm fine. You weren't even here."

She pulled her shoulders up. "You're right." She looked at him, a hollow stare surrounded by her pale features. "I better get back. We're not done."

He let her go as she started to walk away. He stopped in his tracks as a beam of sunlight flashed through the trees and landed on her hair.

It glowed a pale white blonde with dark yellow streaks. His heart stilled for what felt like an eternity as he made the unbelievable connection. His brain wanted to deny it, but...

"Selene!" Her name came out in a shocked croak. She turned to look at him, composed once more. Her face was unreadable in the shadows and playing light. When her look became questioning when he remained silent, he simply shook his head. "Nothing. Never mind." But his heart was pounding like a drum against his chest, and his tongue suddenly felt too large for his mouth.

It wasn't possible, was it? How was the wolf always around with Selene only a few minutes behind? His mind told him it couldn't be, it wasn't possible.

As he worked in one observation room at the hospital, prepping a broken leg for a cast, Selene was in surgery stitching a woman up who had suffered glass lacerations. He knew where she was constantly now. It was unnerving.

Gradually as he worked through several victims from the pileup, he convinced himself it was a freak accident, a chance of nature. Maybe he had a guardian angel now, an angel in the shape of a pale wolf. There was no logical way it could be her, or her being it.

"Doctor?"

"Yes?"

"Are we finished?"

He looked up from his stool where he sat examining the patient's legs. "Yes, sorry." He gave his best doctor smile. "You're all done." He stood, pushing the simple black padded stool into the corner. "Let me get you some crutches, and you'll be free to go."

The young man gave him a grateful smile. With a bandaged ankle and some raw marks on his shoulder, he had gotten out of the pileup relatively unscathed. This was his last patient from the accident victims needing more than a band-aid.

Fifteen minutes later, he was sitting in his office, his door partially closed, but it didn't take long for it to open again. "Bram? Can I talk to you?"

He gazed up at her, her hair straightened once more, her blouse returned to normal under a clean lab coat. "Sure." He waved to one of the chairs in front of him.

He was surprised to see so much in her expression. He'd never witnessed her being less than professional at the hospital. He didn't want to think about how she was away from work. It made her too accessible, too human.

"What can I do for you?"

She gave him a concerned smile. "I was going to ask you the same thing." Her gaze was dark, keeping her thoughts private as he patiently waited. He leaned in a little over his desk. In his office, so close, she was tempting.

"I was concerned you might have suffered a shock from the gun being pulled on you. If you want to take a few minutes or even longer, it's perfectly acceptable."

He steepled his fingers as he contemplated her. "You know, I could almost say the same thing to you." But her face remained expressionless. He knew the idea was preposterous, and she showed no reaction to his words. Not that he was honestly expecting one. When she remained impassive, he said, "I'm fine. You've had more recent experiences, far more dangerous."

She did have the decency to lower her gaze. "I know," she said in a small voice. "But that was my fault." Gray eyes were tormented when she lifted her head, staring right into him. "If anything had happened to you..." He watched as she pulled herself in, tightening her control.

"But it didn't. I guess he had a hallucination or something. He was so loaded, it's a surprise he was even standing."

She nodded once, everything about her once more guarded. She stood from the chair. "I'm glad you're okay," she said quietly as she started for the door.

"Selene?" He didn't move, could hardly breathe.

"Yes?" Her hand rested on the door, ready to flee was what came to his mind.

He stood with an entranced slowness, the ache of wanting her right under his skin. "Thank you."

She nodded once and then, like a wraith, disappeared from sight.

* * * *

Selene ran for miles that night. Today had been too close, and she still felt on edge. When she'd neared the frozen tableau and had seen the gun, she'd lost all reason. She was too slight to even think of overpowering a full-grown male stoned out of his mind on who knew what. It was the only conclusion she could come to in a split-second decision.

She didn't regret it. How could she? But it only marked the widening gulf that had begun to build between her and Bram. She knew he wanted her. God, she wanted him so badly it was worse than a constant heat in her. A persistent need that hummed in her blood, like the simmering of a volcano.

She realized he would never accept it after that afternoon. He'd come up with more excuses than a tardy school boy, not that she could blame him. She wasn't normal. She wasn't typical. She wasn't human.

She snorted as she flopped down in the sun-heated grass, watching the moon make its traversed path over the night sky. Well, she *was* human. She was just different. She closed her eyes as her breathing lightened, listening to the night owl screech overhead. *Different was a mild way of putting it,* she told herself sarcastically. She couldn't speak, but she could definitely talk to herself.

She'd been swamped with an intense fear unlike anything she'd ever known that afternoon. One she didn't know how to define, or how to make go away. If Bram had been hurt... She couldn't even think about it, and he'd already done so much for her. She lay there, unable to make a single muscle move, weary from the constant emotional battle.

Much later, she rolled over and hefted herself to her feet. Maybe she should call Roman. She was lost, confused, scared. He'd already lived through all of these emotions, all of the trials of making a life with a mate. With his love.

She jerked to a stop midstride. *Love?* Was she in love with Bram? *Oh, hell.* It made her want to cry more, to howl like a wild wind. She didn't know what love was supposed to be like, feel like, when it came to a mate. Confusion over love and mates was something she didn't know how to deal with.

Her head and tail drooped by the time she reached the clearing. She sniffed the air and the earth only to freeze, stock still.

Her head rose slowly and there he stood, his brown hair mussed like he'd raked his hand through it. His gaze bore into her when it landed on her. She'd been so deep in her misery, she'd walked into plain sight, too far from the comforting shadows of the woods.

She started to back up, to hide in the woods, until he left. She couldn't do this. A friendship would have to be enough.

"Wait!" The one word reached her like so many years before, and now as then, she stilled, unable to ignore the plea. She watched him shove away from his Explorer, taking a few tentative steps in her direction. Questions flitted over his face, the doubts, the disbelief.

"This isn't possible." His voice cracked as he stared without blinking once. She felt a flare of hope when he didn't turn and run, and her head lifted higher. She hadn't dared to move closer. What was the point? The next move was Bram's.

His throat worked as his chest heaved, a harsh sound in the darkness surrounding them with a surreal silence. The quiet was sliced to shreds in the next instant when his gaze hardened. He frowned at her, his fists clenched at his sides. His voice was rough but sure. "No. This isn't possible." Anger began to brighten his gaze. Anger at himself for allowing his imagination to try to lead him to what she needed him to believe was possible. "You're her dog, *only* a dog," he snapped, his eyes flashing in the moonlight with pulsating mistrust.

She didn't wait for his next outburst but fled into the trees, running as fast as her heartbroken legs would take her.

* * * *

"What do you mean?" Bram stared at Priss in disbelieving shock at what he'd heard.

"She called this morning and said she'd be gone for a few days." Priss tamped down the pages she held, preparing a patient file.

"Just like that?" He practically snarled it, not understanding why it mattered so much. It was not like her to disappear with such little notice.

She didn't even blink an eye. "We have help if we need it. She wouldn't have left without ensuring that. She knows how to run this place," she purposely reminded him. After a heartbeat, she shared, "She sounded stressed and extremely upset on the phone." The concern in her voice was clear now.

Bram leaned over the counter, trying to keep his voice lowered. "Did she say anything else? I know they're having problems with a poacher out near her cabin."

Priss shook her head. "Even if she were, she wouldn't say anything about it. She handles her problems." She finally looked up at him. "Doctor, I've been here as long as she has. I've never heard her sound like this." It was the only hint that she was as surprised by Selene's vanishing act as he was.

He offered an optimistic smile, camouflaging his own worries. "I'm sure she'll be fine. If she calls in, let me know. I'd like to know if she's okay."

She nodded, once again the calm and collected duty nurse who held the floors together. She was as strong as Selene. No wonder they worked well together. With that thought, he left to make his rounds. Two days later he got a call, but it wasn't from Selene.

"Just a minute, Morgan. He's right here." Priss put the call on hold. "Dr. Benedetti, Morgan Aiza is on the phone."

"Tell him Selene is at home," he said without looking up from the report in his hand.

"I did, but he wants to talk to you. He can't find her."

His head snapped up from the pages he was reviewing, but he didn't have a reply. Where was she if she wasn't at home?

"Transfer it to my office, please." He flipped through the pages in front of him, then with a nod left the file on her desk and strode for his office.

He picked up the phone as he pushed the door closed, an eerie, unsettled feeling knifing him.

"Hi, Doc. Morgan here. I know you're busy, but I need a favor."

"Yes?" he answered cautiously. That eerie feeling turned to dread.

"I'm at the Washington state line checking on logging infractions or I would do this myself, but I can't reach Selene."

He let out a small sigh of relief. "I'm sure she's nearby. She took some time off," he informed Morgan, ready to dismiss the whole conversation.

Morgan was silent for several stretched-out seconds. "Dr. Benedetti, I've talked with her. You were at her cabin on Tuesday night and she told me she saw you. I haven't been able to reach her since then." His voice dripped with brotherly concern. "Look, she was hurt. She felt rejected."

"Wait! What the hell are you talking about?" He pushed on his door with a foot, ensuring it was firmly closed. "I didn't see her, I saw her dog. This huge, wolf-looking dog."

Morgan's laugh was biting. "Bram, you're an idiot. That was no dog. She's tried more times than I can say to show you, to tell you." Morgan grumbled under his breath. "I'm making it worse. Look, see if she's still there. I told her to try to be more impulsive, and I think she may have taken it too literally. I've never lost track of either of the girls, and now I can't find Selene."

Bram lifted his gaze heavenward. "It's only Thursday, she's due back on Saturday."

"Dr. Benedetti." Morgan paused as a large vehicle passed in the background. "Damn semis," he groused darkly. "Look, all I'm asking is check to see if she's still there. The phone is ringing off the hook, and I'm too far away."

"What do you mean still there? Why would she leave?" He leaned against his desk, completely confused.

"You don't really want me to answer that, do you?" Morgan asked, a silken threat right under his words.

"I really don't know what you are talking about," he replied in an exasperated tone. "There is nothing going on between us, and I know I haven't seen her since her last day here."

Bram frowned deeply as Morgan cursed into the earpiece. "You're a piece of work, doctor. She's never been wrong, until now." He cursed again, an angry barb that was a direct hit. Bram flinched at the cold tone on the phone. "Never mind. I'll find her when I get home on Sunday." And the phone went dead in his hand.

He dropped the phone to its cradle with stiff fingers and he rounded his desk. Without thinking about why he was doing it, he flipped through his card holder and found her home number. He punched the buttons and waited for the expected answer, but after ten rings, he had to agree that she wasn't there.

He set the phone down a second time, a little less exasperated, maybe. It looked like Morgan's concern wasn't unfound. Where was she? What was going on? And what the hell was Morgan so mad about? He stripped out of his lab coat and laid it over the back of his chair. He could at least go look. Now he was growing concerned. Morgan's concern was only adding fire to an already burning worry. Disappearing was not Selene's style.

He stopped at the counter briefly. "Priss, Dr. Dave is on duty tonight. If you need me or have any problems, call me. I have an errand to run, then I'll be home this evening."

She looked up at him, blinking those blue eyes of hers like it was not unusual for him to leave during the middle of the day. "Sure. I'll have Kimberly do a walkthrough if she hasn't already started."

He tried to smile calmly, forcing his deepening concerns to stay locked up tight. "Thanks. See you in the morning."

She only nodded as he hurried out. He lifted his keys from his pocket nearing his Explorer. It was a better vehicle for the area than the little sports car he'd owned in St. Louis. He laughed once as he pictured the little red two-door buried under a snowdrift. It wouldn't have taken much.

On the drive to Selene's, he wondered why he was doing it. He wasn't going to let whatever this was between them go any further. He could forget about the kisses. If he tried really hard, he could. Really, really hard.

He snorted a disgusted sound, his hands twisting on the steering wheel in agitation. Okay, so he was lying to himself about forgetting them, but it didn't matter. He would find her, tell her to call her brother before he sent out search parties, and then go home.

He killed the engine in the front clearing next to her Jeep. So she was somewhere nearby. He searched through his windshield for signs of life or of the dog but saw nothing. The cabin looked dark from the outside. In fact, the whole clearing was silent. No birds, no breeze. It raised the eerie chill he'd first felt several notches when he'd picked up the phone in his office. He got out of his SUV.

"Selene!" He called and waited, but there was nothing. He slammed his door, annoyed that he was letting this get to him so much. Morgan had gotten into his head, that's all. She was a grown woman. There wasn't anything to worry about.

He marched up to the porch and knocked. His chest tightened painfully when the door glided open under his hand. He edged it wider, poking in his head. "Selene?" His voice held a soft echo for a split second. That eerie feeling doubled.

His sight was aided by the fainter sunlight flooding the cabin as he searched. Nothing appeared to have been disturbed as he closed the door behind him. Seeing that offered a small reprieve of relief. He passed by the kitchen with barely a glance. Something he couldn't name told him he wouldn't find her there. He called again, consciously aware she wouldn't answer. She wasn't there.

His gaze landed on the bedroom door hanging half open. Instantly his memory recalled the last time he'd been on the other side of that door. Her bared shoulder, her softly tousled hair, her face warmed with a blush that he hadn't tried to feel drawn to, but could remember well now.

He gritted his teeth, fighting the memory down as he took careful steps to reach the door. He knew she was not in the house. That much was obvious, but his hand still shook as he pushed on the door. He didn't want to surprise anyone who may have been there unwanted, if they hadn't heard him already. The door swung open.

There was no way to prepare himself for what he found.

He felt his world spin as he took in the carnage. "Oh God. Selene!"

Chapter Eight

Her bed had been stripped with a clawed hand, all the bedding piled onto the floor in a mass of blood and woman. His voice cracked in brittle shock. "Dear God, what happened?" But there was no answer. He slipped to his knees, crawling carefully to reach her. He found her pulse. A bare thread of life. Relief crashed through him as he sagged in place. "God, how long have you been like this?" he whispered, his heart in his throat, unable to move for the first time in his life as he stared.

He didn't know where to begin as he took in her wounds and injuries. Her palms were shredded, the blood long since dried to a dark red umber crust. There was a long gash that gaped for several deep inches across her calf, bared to the bone, and if he hadn't already seen it happen once he wouldn't have believed he was looking at another bullet hole in her side, below her ribs. She was scratched from head to toe; there wasn't an inch of her body that didn't show some sign of damage.

"Jesus, woman, when you look for trouble you really know how to find it, don't you?" he said, his harsh breathing a graveled rasp in the room's silence. His feet were unsteady as he rose and jogged into the living room, dragging in gulps of air to get a fast grasp on his bearings.

He quickly called the hospital and gave them a change of plans. He looked over his shoulder. He desperately wanted to take her in, but he knew there would be too many questions by people who knew her for those kinds of injuries. Fighting for a deeper calm, he marched to his vehicle to gather his medical travel bag, locking her front door on his return to her room.

He lifted her as carefully as he could to the bed. She didn't flinch or even moan. He brushed stray hair away from her pale face, forcing his hand to stay steady as he looked once more, mapping out the course of action for her wounds in his head.

He washed his hands as he mentally did a list, and as if he were in a surgical theatre instead of her simple bedroom, he set to work. He started with the ugly gash on her leg, cleaning it where the jagged, torn skin and flesh made a good suture near impossible. He winced for her when he flooded the open wound, grinding his teeth when he washed away the old blood, until fresh color began to appear. The white shine of bone against the newly pinked surface of flesh was a startling contrast. He forced his hands to remain firm as he made a web of loose stitches.

The bullet was next. The way it had lodged itself, it wasn't anywhere as hard to work out as the first one had been. It wasn't deep but had entered at an angle and had cracked a rib on the way. No matter what she said, she was going to be in pain when she woke up. He lifted a shoulder to wipe his brow as he meticulously continued to work, unaware of the passage of time, unaware of anything other than the woman who lay under his touch.

He shifted to the next of her wounds, taking in the rough treatment of her hands. He shook his head as he wondered what she could have possibly been doing to get this cut up. The question evaporated when he knew he couldn't even begin to answer it.

Once her hands were clean, he discovered a long gash down the center of her palm that miraculously had stopped before her wrist and the arteries that lay within. It was almost as severe as the gash on her leg.

He was slow, methodical with his ministrations, cleansing, drying, stitching, until the last thing he had to do was wrap them to help keep them clean.

He shook out the sheet he had found her on, his gaze widening as he saw the holes that had been ripped through it and the blood that was everywhere. He tore small, mostly clean strips from the sheets, wrapping her hands with tender care.

He worked through the afternoon, caring for her with sure and steady fingers until he was finally able to straighten at the bedside and manage a sigh of relief. Looking out the window, he found it was well after dark. He took a few minutes to double check everything from sutures to bleeding and then covered her with a fresh blanket. He would have to move her soon. The bed was ruined.

He froze on a turned heel when he realized he was going to have to stay with her. Morgan was away, and he didn't have any idea who to reach for her. Okay, he could do that. He turned on a lamp next to her bed, turning off the bedroom light then went to the kitchen. Maybe he could make a broth or something for her. She'd need water soon, and if she didn't get a fever she was going to wake up needing something for nourishment.

When he opened the refrigerator, he was surprised to see a few packages of beef, bacon, and eggs and very little of anything else, as in nothing else. He closed the door, popped open the freezer, and stood in stunned silence. It was packed with red meat, from steaks to strips.

"Do you only eat meat?" he wondered. "How can a body live on that?" He closed the freezer again. Food wasn't the first thing on his list at the moment, either. The only thing he could do was be close by and wait.

He went to the living room and noticed something he had missed when he had entered. The painting of the pale wolf was gone. There was an empty hole on the wall where it had hung. He felt an ominous shiver slide down his spine as he stared at the blank space.

When the phone rang, he jumped, his heart shooting through his ribs. "Dr. Benedetti." Then, on a shaky breath, he corrected himself. "Sorry, Dr. Aiza's residence."

"It's Morgan." His response was clipped. "What are you doing there?" The note of angry distrust was clear even over miles and miles of phone wires.

Bram felt exhaustion creep up on him as he pinched the bridge of his nose. The hours he spent bent over Selene hit him like a sledgehammer. He fought the exhaustion from slurring his words as he said, "You asked for me to come check on her."

Morgan's silence was short-lived. "Did you find her?" Bram relented when Morgan's anxious concern filled every syllable.

Bram sank down to the couch that lined the wall below the windows. "Yes, I found her." His head fell forward, held in a tired hand.

"Why doesn't that sound like a good thing?" Morgan asked quietly. "Where is she?"

"She's hurt. I don't know what happened. I found her on the floor of her bedroom torn to shreds. She's resting in her bed, but I doubt she's going to be happy when she wakes up. Someone took one of her paintings."

Morgan's tone was immediately wary. "What painting?"

"I noticed it a few minutes ago. The pale wolf is gone."

"Oh God," he groaned in an agonized voice. Bram was taken by surprise at the emotion in those two words. Then Morgan asked, "You didn't take her to the hospital, did you?" Morgan's voice had spiked as if the idea had just occurred to him.

"No, the injury questions would have been too hard to answer." *Not to mention her ability to heal.*

"Among others," Morgan replied, almost in agreement with Bram's thoughts. His voice was agitated with worry. "Look, I can't get out of here until Saturday at the earliest. Sunday is more likely. If you need to leave, call Roman. His number's in her book on her bed stand. Brooke is still out of the country, and he's closest."

Bram's gaze swept to the partially open bedroom doorway. "No. I'll stay. I'll get someone to cover the watch at the hospital." He had until morning to find someone at least.

"All right," he allowed himself to say, only a small concession of relief in his voice. "One other thing."

"Yes?" The hair on Bram's neck had stood up at the tone of warning in his voice.

"The meat."

Bram made a note of disgust. "How can she live on that?"

"Doc, you still don't get it, do you?" When Bram remained silent, Morgan continued. "Warm and very, very rare. She'll heal faster if she eats."

"You're kidding, right?"

Morgan snarled across the miles between them. "If you can't do it, then call Roman. She needs someone there who cares if she lives." The slam of the phone was harsh in his ear.

He stared at the phone in his hand in disbelief. It wasn't possible, was it? His gaze traveled across the room again, landing on the blank spot that once held the painting. He hung up the phone with a twisted feeling in his stomach.

He shook his head minutes later and rose to check on his patient. Her pulse was growing stronger, and she wasn't showing any signs of fever yet, knowledge he met with a hesitant sense of relief. He checked her pressure and was thankful to see it was leveling off. She'd lost a lot of blood, and he'd been worried.

As he stood over her, he brushed the hair away from her face again, careful of the scratches that had not been major considering what he'd had to work on. He stayed with her for some time watching her sleep.

It didn't matter how many days had passed since their last kiss, he still wanted her with a burning need that wasn't letting go or lessening on any level. What had hit him as he stared at her resting form was the incredible need to lie with her and offer comfort, to hold her, to ease her pain. As a doctor, he knew that wasn't going to be possible. As a man, he wished it were.

Much later he went to the kitchen, making himself something to ease his own hunger. He looked at his watch to see that it was after nine. He'd left the hospital at three to come find her. An eternity had passed since he walked out those double glass doors.

He slept on the couch, rising once an hour to check on her throughout the night, but she never stirred, unaware of her surroundings. He was stiff, sore, and hungry by the time six o'clock rolled around. He reached the hospital and advised them that he had been paged out for an emergency in the middle of the night and if they needed him for anything to call him. He hung up with them, not knowing if the cell got signal out where he was or not. He knew he wasn't going to tell them he was at Selene's.

He heard a motorcycle shortly after seven and then a heavy tread on the porch. The knock was persistent. He opened it cautiously, aware of what Selene had said of who knew of her house and where she lived. He blinked in the bright morning sunshine as he looked at the man on the porch. At nearly six feet, Bram was not short, but the man on the porch towered over him by at least half a foot.

"You must be Bram Benedetti," the man said in a deep, rumbled voice.

"You could only be Roman." The dark-haired man nodded. "I guess you're the cavalry," Bram muttered. Roman shot him a black-eyed stare. "I told Morgan I could stay with her, and I will." But Bram stepped out of the way to let Selene's brother in. He really didn't want her brother to walk over him.

"That's not why I'm here. Although I would like to know how she is, see her if possible. Morgan said she was hurt pretty badly."

"She was. I have no idea how she got that way, either." He shook his head as they faced one another.

Roman grunted, cutting him down with a sharp gaze. "I believe you. I can tell Morgan was right."

"About what?" Bram snapped, then remembered this was her brother as he glared.

Roman made a low sound in his chest. "You have no idea," was all he said as he turned to march into the bedroom, uncaring if he should or shouldn't. Bram let him go, feeling relief. Was her whole family that intimidating? No wonder she'd never married.

There was silence for a few minutes until he heard his name from her bedroom. "Make nice with the crazy family," he managed under his breath.

Roman had exposed her leg and was staring at the long, garish wound. "You did that?" he asked brusquely, pointing to the stitches. Evidently her brother wasn't a heartless rock. Seeing Selene was bringing him down to earth with a thud.

Bram was kinder when he answered. "It was the best I could do under the circumstances. The skin was too ragged and swollen to suture well."

Roman nodded once. "Well, for an ass, at least you're a good doctor." But he was smiling as he said it.

"I can only assume then that Morgan has already given you his opinion of me," Bram retorted drily.

"Yes, but I reserve my judgments. I believe everyone deserves at least that much," he said as he carefully folded her leg underneath the sheets. "How long has it been since she's eaten?"

"I don't know. I found her unconscious, and she's been out since I've been here."

Roman bowed his head. "She won't heal like this," he said thickly. "She needs to eat."

"I would have fed her at least a broth, but she hasn't woken up long enough to drink water."

Roman's words were anguished as he closed his eyes, his expression tight with pain. "She doesn't want to."

Bram's head swirled. "Doesn't want to? Why would she give up? I know she can heal."

Roman's look rocked him from the other side of the bed. "She's done everything she could to help you figure it out." Roman looked down once more at his sister, then with a laser-eyed stare left the room. Bram could only follow, closing the door gently behind him.

Roman had stopped in the middle of the room staring at the wall adorned with the paintings, and one open space that didn't look balanced.

"Do you know anything about wolves?" he said, calmer but with a thoughtful undertone.

"Some. Why?"

Roman's next exhalation was a forceful sound in the silence of the cabin. "When I met Del—Delilah—I didn't know what to do. She drove me crazy, and not always in a good way. She still does." He offered a rueful smile. "The only difference was I didn't let our secret out until much later. Selene tries to be sensible, but when someone she cares about is threatened, she will do anything to protect them. She's done that for you. I know you've made the connection, or you wouldn't have even noticed or cared that the painting was gone. We all feared for her, for when this time of her life would come." He crossed muscled arms as he contemplated the wall. "Did you know that wolves mate for life?"

"Yes," he answered with a touch of tired impatience. He didn't need a lesson in animal monogamy. "I've heard that many times. But what that has to do with me—"

"That's what I'm trying to tell you. Irrevocably, she must tell you herself. I know you don't want to believe. Do you know who those are?" He tossed a pointed look at the remaining paintings.

"Who?" His confusion was right there in the one word.

"I didn't stutter," Roman snapped. "Do you know why the one is missing?"

"I noticed it was gone after I had stitched her up. I assumed someone had stolen it, but I get the feeling you're going to tell me something completely different." He swallowed once, slowly. Whatever it was, he had a gut feeling he wasn't prepared for the truth.

Roman turned to face him over his shoulder. "I'm going to give you a bit of advice, something I wish someone had done for me. Give it a chance. Let yourself believe." He faced the wall again. "I can only tell you she took it down because it is her statement. She came home to die."

"To die?" he said, feeling his words like a physical blow to his gut.

Roman placed a kind hand on his shoulder. "What do you feel you should do for her? What is your heart telling you to do?"

Bram trembled as his gaze swung to the bedroom door, where she was lying wounded, helpless. "I want to hold her. It's irrational; I can't stop the pain."

Roman smiled at him. "It's not irrational. Let her know you do care, however much it is. I'm asking as a brother, please don't let her die."

"To die?" he whispered, still reeling. "I think Morgan is expecting me to leave now that you are here." Bram's head was spinning.

Roman made a disgusted, impatient sound. "Morgan is the oldest and a royal pain, and he looks out for the girls with a vengeance." Roman caught Bram's gaze as he stepped for the front door. "But I can't stay. Del is due to deliver any day now." Roman shot him a huge grin as he opened the door. "See? Many things are possible if you believe." And before he could argue, the door had shut between them and seconds later he heard the rumble of Roman's motorcycle outside, receding quickly into the quiet morning.

"Hell, I'm as crazy as they are," Bram mumbled under his breath, but he'd heard and recognized the plea in Roman's words. He wasn't going to let her die. Not on his watch.

* * * *

Selene turned her head and found warmth. Skin. The scent tickled her nose as it wrapped around her mind. Half delirious with pain, she knew she was imagining it. She fought the urge to cry out when she shifted. Damn, but she hurt everywhere. She inhaled once more and found the heated scent again. She felt the movement of breathing against her hair, an arm resting against her.

Her mind couldn't break apart the signals. Where was she? Why did she hurt? She shifted her body a little higher, and found the source of the warm scents. The animal flicked out its tongue touching, tasting; the woman knew she should have been alone.

She had come home to die.

"Mmm," a sleepy male voice said in a purr. "Are you awake?"

She tried to swallow but had nothing to force down her throat. The weight next to her moved as a cup came to rest on her lips. She sipped, thankful for any moisture.

Her eyes snapped open as a ravenous hunger clawed at her with the first sip. The cup held a flavorful beef broth. She finished it in three swallows. She relaxed backward again, realizing she had lifted herself several inches from the bed.

"I guess you're among us again," the kind voice said.

She licked her lips, savoring the flavor, then sighed as her eyes fluttered to focus. "Bram?" she croaked, dazed and in pain.

"Yes." He looked down at her with a soft smile. "You gave me a hell of a scare, lady. Do you always go out to find that much trouble, or was it a lucky night for you?"

Her eyes felt heavy. "How long... What happened?"

The bed gave way when he rose from it. "Food, then talk," he ordered.

She drifted in and out of consciousness until a familiar smell reached her nose. It was warm as it touched her lips. She took it and swallowed it in a few bites. Her eyes popped open in surprise. Meat! He was feeding her meat.

She ate like a starving body, chunks of warmed red meat a piece at a time, the blood still dripping as he hand-fed her from the bedside. When the plate was empty he set it on the nightstand, wiping her mouth and chin with a napkin to wipe his own hands after.

She felt warm and relaxed until she tried to move and cried out in a sharp yelp.

"Be still," he reprimanded. "You're torn to shreds."

She closed her eyes again. "How long have you been here?"

"Two days now. Morgan asked me to check on you when he couldn't reach you."

"Worried sick. That's Morgan," she whispered. Her body ached even as she felt warmth as the food—pure protein—hit her system.

"With good reason." He brushed a length of hair away from her face with a gentle touch. "Do you want to tell me what happened?"

Her heart sank when she remembered why she had done something so foolish. "Does it matter?"

"I don't know," he said truthfully. "But I think it might help me understand why you were on the floor more dead than alive when I found you."

"I should have died," she said with conviction. "I wanted to die." She opened her eyes with an accusing glare.

"I know, and I know why."

"Then why didn't you let me die?" she demanded, her voice weak and unable to hide the wounded woman behind it.

He moved from his spot beside the bed, stretching out next to her with tender care. "Wake me when you're hungry again." He crossed his arm over her body, careful of any soreness. "Rest. You can be mad at me later."

Her body shuddered as his warmth blanketed her, Bram's familiar longed-for scent filling her, comforting her. She fought it. She'd been wrong about him. He didn't want to believe, and if he refused, then he would never care, or love.

She felt him fall asleep next to her, his breathing even and deep against her hair. Her eyes drifted closed, unable to fight the bone-deep weariness caused by the pain.

Especially in her injured condition, she couldn't control the urges that his nearness brought out of her. It didn't matter, she reminded herself. She'd been wrong. That was the sad thought that stayed with her as she fell into sleep.

The sun had moved higher the next time she opened her eyes, but she was alone in bed. So he had left, or maybe it had been her imagination. She wouldn't have been surprised. She turned over and felt the sharp pain in her left leg, the ache in her side. She closed her eyes briefly as the memories came to her. She should be dead, and she knew it.

The door slid open and Bram walked to the edge of the bed, sitting in the chair he had used earlier in the day. "Are you hungry? Thirsty?" he asked as he placed a tray on the stand next to her bed.

"Why are you here?" she demanded quietly, still unwilling to look at him.

"Making sure you don't die. Please don't make Roman mad at me by dying," he begged in a jesting voice. "You weren't kidding. He's huge!" He smiled when she bit her lip.

She shrugged. "I guess I'm used to him."

"Give me your hands," he ordered, reaching with open palms.

She pulled them slowly from beneath the covers. He unwrapped one and then the other, turning them this way and that as he studied them. "You don't need the bandages for these any longer, but I'm going to watch that slice. The recovery has been a little slower since you haven't been able to eat."

She shot him a look. How did he know that?

"Are you my doctor?"

"Yes, so be a good patient." He lifted the corner of her sheet. "Push out your leg." She did as he told her. "Hmm, also slow, but this was really bad. No leg waxing for a while." He grinned when she tried not to laugh. He moved to the other side and lifted the sheet, baring her side. "See, that's almost healed. Damn, I wish I could do that. I hate shaving nicks," he sighed with a disgusted shrug. Her smile was unstoppable.

"Take a deep breath." She did. "Do your ribs hurt?" She shook her head and laughed outright when he mockingly glared at her. She swallowed it before he could hear the moan her laughter had brought on herself. He did have a great bedside manner, but she'd known that. "You had a cracked rib from the bullet. I think I could almost hate you for that." But he was grinning as he retook his seat. "Do you think you can sit up to eat?"

"Yeah, I think so." He propped her up as he padded her pillows, then set down the tray on her lap.

"I wasn't sure if you used forks and stuff with the raw meat, so I cut it up for you," he said.

"I usually do…" And before she had finished, he had whipped out a fork from behind his back. "Oh, Bram."

"Eat, then cry, or yell, or whatever it is you do after you almost die. We still need to talk, and I need to call in again."

Her heart hit her ribs at her own selfish behavior. "Oh God, the hospital!"

He put a reassuring hand on her shoulder. "They still think you're on personal time, and they think I'm doing house calls. Thank God for Dr. Dave and the others. They can call me on the cell if they really need me, and I've been checking in constantly. Before you panic, no one knows about this and no one suspects, I hope, that I'm here." He stood from the chair, pointing to the tray on her lap. "Eat; doctor's orders." She felt her eyes fill as he walked out the door.

She looked at the plate. Twice now he'd brought rare, warmed, red meat. Her gaze flicked to the door. What had happened? How did he know? She ate a little slower than the first time while she tried to figure him out, but the plate was still cleaned before he entered the room again, long before she had an answer to his new attitude.

He lifted an eyebrow when he returned moments later. "I guess there's a reason you keep your freezer stocked."

She glanced bashfully at the cleaned plate. "Only when I need it; otherwise, I eat like everyone else. Almost," she offered when his eyes teasingly lifted to hers. "Have you been eating?"

He nodded. "Although, if this gets to be a regular thing, a couple of potatoes go a long way with steak. You know, for variety," he said with a nonchalant rolled shoulder.

He took the tray and moved it out of the way. She watched him cautiously as he sat, this time on the side of the bed close to her. He lifted a hand to cradle her face as his eyes locked on her. She wanted to melt. He felt so good, so right. But then she remembered his anger, his disbelief, and straightened her shoulders. Better to do this now, a clean break, rather than draw it out.

"Bram, I appreciate this—"

He pressed a gentle finger to her mouth.

"Wait," he interrupted her gently. "There is something that I have to do first." His voice caressed over her spine, sending tingles shooting over her body. She waited with an expectant breath as he leaned forward. Was he going to kiss her? She felt her heart jump hard against her ribs as the thought of his lips stirred her blood.

He gripped the sides of her head as his gaze darkened, to tilt her until her throat was bared, arched to his touch. Before she knew what he had planned, he swept his tongue from her collarbone to her jaw in a long, languid trail of heat. He nipped the underside of her jaw as a final measure. It was the most erotic sensation she'd ever encountered. She groaned when he settled close to her ear.

"Consider yourself marked, lady," he murmured against her skin.

She shivered in his hold, unable to stop the response and almost scared by its strength. "You don't have to do this. I understand." Her breath hitched with a pulsing reaction as he nipped her ear, silencing her argument. Trying to give him his freedom was killing her, especially since he seemed to be missing the obvious effort entirely.

"No, you don't, because I'm just beginning to." He sighed against the column of her neck. "Roman pointed out a few things for me," he told her tenderly.

"He was really here?" she asked as she fought to control the racing shivers that stole over her. She thought she had imagined his visit.

"Yesterday morning, for a few minutes."

"But Delilah?"

He kneaded the back of her head. "That's why he couldn't stay." He kissed the corner of her mouth. "He loves you very much and wanted to see how you were. News travels fast in your family's grapevine."

Her shoulders sagged in disappointment. "He's using you. I won't kill myself. I'm too tired and sore to try. You can leave, Bram. I don't need a babysitter."

His gaze darkened, mesmerizing as he stared at her. "You have no idea what I've been through in the last two days. Hell, for the last week, but I admitted something to myself this morning after holding you all night, whether you want to believe it or not, I do care. Maybe not enough to be your mate, as Roman tried to explain it, but you do matter." She watched as his eyes began to glitter with heat. "So, do I need to mark you again? Because I could really get into that."

A smile tugged at the corner of her mouth and she cleared her throat, actually feeling a little shy. "Really? Maybe you should, you know, practice? Because I could help you with it." Her grin was obliterated with a moan as he did exactly that.

Chapter Nine

A few minutes after a thorough marking lesson, he carried her wrapped body into the living room. He eased her to the couch, tucking her under an extra blanket to rest while he cleaned up in the kitchen. She flipped through channels on the TV, but there wasn't anything to catch her interest for long.

She scooted forward to let him slide in behind her, pulling her to rest in comfort against his chest. She closed her eyes as the warmth of his body enveloped her, his arms wrapping around her to hold her gently, conscious of her body's aches and soreness. He lifted her hands, checking them, and once he was satisfied, curled his around them.

"So why don't you tell me how this happened?" He caressed the top of her hands with his thumbs, sending sparks up and down her spine with the casual touch.

"I don't know where to start," she admitted.

"Tell me this first. When did you take the painting down?" he asked, a soft undercurrent in his words that vibrated through his chest, something that said he already knew the answer.

"Tuesday night, after you left."

"But I didn't see you," he denied lowly. Firm but not enough to call her a liar.

"I don't know how to convince you, but yes, you did."

She felt his head fall forward, his arms tightening as he railed against reality. His tension became a palpable stiffness between them.

"It's all right," she finally said. "I can't expect you to believe or to understand."

He adjusted them both, pulling her closer. "Roman said it was your secret to tell. The meat. The fast healing. Did he mean what I think he meant?" It was a low-voiced question, edging on a quiver of apprehension.

"Tell me," she whispered, too scared to hope.

He twisted to face the wall to stare directly at the blank space. "That was really you," he said in a breathy voice. "All those years ago. The day of the wreck. The other night," he said with a final whisper below her ear.

"Are you asking, or saying?"

"I wish I knew," he admitted. "Why can't you tell me I'm wrong, or prove me right?"

"Because I won't. I can't prove you wrong, and I won't lead you to where you don't want to go."

He took a deep breath. "And if I want to know? Want to see the real you?"

"Bram..." It was a helpless feeling, being torn between two worlds.

"Prove me right, Selene," he begged gently into her ear, a soft caress that sizzled through her.

Terror kept her from swimming headfirst into the joy his words brought. "Only my mate should see me that way."

She felt his first real hesitation, but it was short-lived.

"One step at a time, okay?"

"It's a huge risk for me." She clutched his fingers in hers.

"Because you're hurt?" he asked, instantly concerned.

"No. Because I have to trust you."

He rubbed his cheek over her hair. "Selene, no matter what happens, you can always and forever trust me."

She took a deep breath and felt his encouragement. "All right, but if you faint, I can't help you." *Or me.*

She unsteadily reached her feet, leaving the blankets he'd covered her with behind on the couch. Heat flushed her skin as his gaze took in her body, sweeping over her bruised and sore shape, and still finding her desirable.

Holding her weight on her one good leg, she searched for the inner warmth and prayed she wasn't too weak to do the change, in either direction. She called on the heat, feeling it bloom, feeling for her heart, listening to the changing tempo in her racing blood. She closed her eyes, gasping as pain seared through her, engulfed her, but it was too late to stop. Stopping would only prolong her agony. When she had changed before, she had been delirious with pain. The pain the change had created on her body then hadn't been a drop of water in a bucket.

This time her body argued every single twitch and made sure she knew it. She was panting by the time she rested on four paws, looking up at a frozen, pale Bram.

Damn! She knew it. She closed her eyes as her head sagged. She'd laid herself on the line and lost. Her leg throbbed, ached. She'd forgotten about the stitches. They didn't take the transformation as well. She'd never been injured like this before. If this was any indication, she wouldn't forget anytime soon.

Waiting for some sign, her pain was nothing compared to the blank, still quiet stare she was receiving. It was too late. She was tired and would need to rest before she could reverse the change, at least for a few minutes. Then the fact that Bram knew would have to be dealt with.

Her head drooped further and her tail brushed the floor in dejection. She was taken by surprise when he slid from the couch to kneel in front of her.

"You're beautiful," he whispered reverently.

Her head picked up as her heart thundered in her chest, scared to really hope, terrified to believe now that it was happening in front of her. His hand slowly stretched out and sank into her ruff, and her eyes closed in pure enjoyment. Her tail twitched once, twice, and he laughed.

"You're absolutely incredible," he said as his smile broadened. "Can you understand me?" She caught his gaze and clicked her teeth.

His laugh was shaky. "I remember that. All those years ago, it was *you* I saw." She lifted her head to rub against his arm. "I really thought after I'd seen you at the creek, I'd turned you into a vision. You saved me."

There were so many things she wanted to tell him, but couldn't.

"Can I touch you, feel you?" he asked, his gaze filled with wonder.

She carefully limped forward on her injured leg, and waited. She arched into his hands rubbing down her spine, heard his murmur of pleasure as his fingers furrowed through her coat. He sighed with discovery as he brushed his face against her shoulder.

"You're the most amazing woman I've ever known," he told her. Her tail wagged again. She wasn't too proud for an occasional compliment. "There's so much to ask, to say," he said a few minutes later. "Can you change?"

She dropped her head, shaking it, then looked at her injured leg.

"It hurt?" he asked her, instantly concerned as his fingers brushed over her tender lower leg. He nodded when she clicked her teeth. "Selene, I had no idea. I didn't want to hurt you."

She pushed her nose against him, not blaming him in the least. She didn't know it would hurt either.

He turned to face her. "Will rest help?" He smiled when she clicked again. "Good thing I finally figured out your language," he teased her. "Can you walk?"

She made a good attempt, but after two hobbling steps he picked her up and carried her. If she'd been able, she would have died of mortification. No one had ever lifted her in that form.

He set her on her feet for a brief minute, stripping the bed and laying out a clean sheet set, saying, "Your bed is ruined, but it will make it a couple more nights."

Her head was sagging with fatigue again when he finally laid her on the bed. She was surprised and warmed when he stretched out along her length. When he draped an arm over her, she dropped a paw over his wrist and felt his answering chuckle.

"I guess when you wake up again, we'll talk and I'll see if I can get one more day out of the visiting surgeon."

And try to come up with some story for their combined absence. That was going to be fun. It was her last thought as sleep overtook her.

* * * *

Bram flipped over and felt fur. His gaze snapped open as he turned his head and found a huge head lying on his outstretched arm. She reached from his arm over the length of the bed, easily five feet long with the tail. He took a steadying breath. Okay, so it hadn't been a dream. Her paw was still resting in his hand, lying in it trustingly.

What she had shown him finally hit home. Her secret. She was a wolf. Her beauty had haunted him, her eyes had always been in his memory, and now, he held her as she slept. He smiled when her paw twitched. Did she dream of chases or of kisses? Warmth flowed through him as he held her, heard a sigh leave her chest as he settled next to her on the mattress. It was a contented sound. His heart beat a steady rhythm as the ramifications of what he was thinking sank in. Not yet, he warned. Some questions still needed to be answered.

He lifted his free hand, focusing to see his watch. God, was it late. He tried to see out the window but only found stars. He'd basically put his life on hold to be there for her. Neither of them had been at the hospital in days. Tongues would soon be gossiping if they weren't already.

He wondered if she had thought about it. Technically she wasn't due back for another day, though he knew she wasn't up to it. Not yet.

He considered the woman he held in his arms. An absolutely amazing creature of life, and from what he could gather, he was her mate. But how did that work, exactly? Were his growing feelings part of the whole mystical soup?

She must have sensed his unease because he felt a wet tongue swipe his arm, a touch of comfort.

"Am I that obvious?" he asked tenderly. "Are you laughing at me?" He was shocked when what he heard sounded very much like laughter a moment later. "Okay, you." He ran a finger over her ribs and felt her squirm. "You better change. We need to talk."

He held his breath as she shimmered in his hold. He felt a brush of something, like a cobweb in a breeze or butterfly wings for a split second as she changed shapes. It was an odd feeling. Not quite uncomfortable, but something he was sure he wasn't supposed to know either.

He relaxed when she let out a relieved sigh. "Did it hurt this time?"

"Only as much as I expected it to," she answered. Her hand had clenched his, her hold strong, until the pain began to subside.

"I didn't want you to hurt," he said as he kissed her shoulder.

"It was a new experience for the both of us. I've never changed with holes in my body that didn't belong there."

"Tacky, sweetheart," he said.

"Sorry." But he heard her smile and knew she wasn't, then her breath caught. "Sweetheart?" she whispered.

"I think I have the right to call you anything I want to now," he said as he nipped at her shoulder, getting a shiver in answer. His body's response was quick, urgent, and very obvious. Belatedly he realized she was naked, which he had forgotten when he'd asked her to change from her wolf form.

"Selene." His voice was hoarse. "I need to get up."

"I understand." Her gaze was shuttered as she rolled away from him. She pulled the sheet up further to cover her nakedness.

"Would you quit saying that?" He slipped away from her, intending to get to his feet, but her next words stopped him.

"Bram, I want you too. I've fought it since day one. And not since the day you came out here. I'm talking six years of wanting."

"This is so fast, I feel like I'm on a roller coaster with you." He couldn't stop his eyes from feasting on her supple form, waiting for him.

"Does it change the way you feel about me? Did yesterday change it?" she asked, and he heard the fearful tremor in her words.

He stretched out with her, pulling her covered body close, uncaring of anything but the frightened heart within the strongest woman he knew. "No, yesterday didn't change it. What you shared made you more incredible for me. More beautiful." His hand shook a little as he brushed her hair, digging for the words. "I've been trying to remember for weeks. Your eyes brought the memory so close, but to find it, I would've had to admit to what I finally saw last night. I could remember that first night, when you were hiding in the trees and you found me. Your eyes." He stared into her gray depths. "They've been with me for years."

He buried his nose in her hair, inhaling the sweet and wild fragrance that was hers. "But you've shocked and scared years out of my life. Let me work this out at my pace."

She pressed herself into him. "Thank you for being honest. That's all I can ask."

He held on for a second longer before he did what his body had been craving for weeks. It was with a great amount of mental effort that he did pull away. "You better dress, if you can. I'll go make us something to drink."

"All right."

He took one last, long look at her body stretched out on the bed and wondered if he'd suddenly gone insane to make himself walk away.

A few minutes later, she joined him, with a slow hobble, in the kitchen where he'd put a kettle on to boil.

"Sorry, I don't do coffee very well. I have good tea, though," she offered as she pulled down two mugs.

"Tea is fine." He leaned against the counter, his arms crossed over his chest as he tried to put everything into perspective. "So, where did you get the injuries? I don't think we ever got around to that."

Her lips lifted in an attempted smile, but it looked rueful. "I had a dumb-luck run-in with the poacher."

His heart clenched painfully in his chest. "Again?"

"Yes." She produced two orbs and filled them with blended loose-leaf tea she kept on her counter, clipping them shut to wait for the water. "I didn't mean to, not at first, but when you left, I wasn't thinking straight. I was confused, angry, feeling rejected. I assumed you had made the connection then. I was being immature about it. I'm the sensible one." She glanced at him, a guilty expression that tore at him. "And I wanted to die. Not so sensible anymore."

The kettle whistle blew and she poured, letting her words sink in. He was constantly in a state of wonder around Selene. "I did have an idea that night, but it was such an incredible idea…"

She lifted a gentle hand to his mouth, silencing him with a tender touch. "It's not necessary. You know the truth, and you're still here. That means more to me right now than you have even guessed at yet," she told him.

"How did you get so hurt? You had lost so much blood." He remembered the condition he'd found her in and had to keep from dragging her into his hold, vowing to never let go again. Instead he turned to see her more fully, trying to keep a restraint on his wants.

He wanted answers first. He'd never get them if he touched her.

"I was trying to circumvent, to get behind him. I'd stumbled on him laying bait, and before I knew it, I was leg deep in a trap."

For the first time, he caught a flicker of fear in her silver-gray gaze as she spoke. "I got out the only way I could. I've never been so careless, but if he saw me... I might as well be dead."

A single tear tracked down her cheek, and he felt his soul rip apart for her. He crushed her into his hold without a single arguable regret. "No. Don't talk like that. Please."

She buried her face into his shoulder, and he felt her whole body shudder. He didn't know what he was going to do, but there was no way a poacher was going to catch the wolf that had stolen his heart.

Chapter Ten

A week later, Selene had successfully returned to work with nothing more than a smile and a dismissively described twisted ankle that had kept her home longer than planned to dissuade any further questions about her limp. She was amazing, and his feelings were still growing.

After she'd been well enough to stay at home alone, he'd returned to his quiet apartment and after five minutes discovered that he didn't like it. There wasn't anything wrong with it, not physically. What he didn't like was not having her with him. In little more than two days with her, holding, touching, and talking, he felt closer to her than he'd ever experienced, ever thought possible, ever wanted.

He was beginning to understand what Roman had been trying to say without giving up the family secret. Wolves mated for life. He was her mate, and he was starting to understand what that meant to his life. He'd been right to not make love to her, not yet, even though his entire body ached for her, craved her. It was a physical pull that drew him deeper and tighter to her.

He couldn't help the little voice that sat on his shoulder, though, the cynical laugh that would remind him of Rebecca and the pain, the humiliation she had brought on him, in the name of love. Was it worth it? He was unwilling to answer that, not yet. That accusing voice was the reason he couldn't take Selene the way he wanted. Until he could give her everything she deserved, until he was able to be hers in every sense, he couldn't shortchange either one of them.

By the time he had his next full day off, she was back to full throttle, running the little clinical hospital with ease. He worried about her and knew she still feared discovery. It was a problem that they would have to face. Whether he accepted what he felt or not, he knew he wasn't going to let someone harm her. That was not an option.

What he found tacked to a pole early that morning was enough to make him see red. Someone had drawn a believable computerized color rendition of the pale wolf and had posted fliers.

Reward. Wild dog hybrid. Attacker. Dangerous to people.

He yanked one down and cursed as he saw many, many more posted around town while he ran his errands. This new predicament sat like a rock in his gut as he tried to think it through, and of course, his day didn't get any better.

Rebecca had found him. When he returned to his apartment, she'd left over ten messages trying to catch him. And as was her style, with each one she'd become increasingly peevish, more demanding. He groaned as he erased them all. He had tried so hard to leave that all behind him. He'd almost allowed himself to believe he had.

His life in Oregon was so much better. He had peace, a challenging position that didn't push him to an early grave, and the beginnings of a relationship that he felt he was finally learning to cope with and not feel like he was a resident of the local padded room club.

He pulled the flier from his pocket and tossed it on the table with an angry glare. Falling to his couch, he rubbed his eyes as he tried to piece it all together.

Selene was in danger. Did the poacher know what she was? Was it the wolf he was after, or had he discovered what they truly were? Were any of the others in danger? Who was this man who was hunting them?

She'd been shot twice, so he obviously had had a clear enough view to see her and to make the drawing. The shots hadn't been life threatening, but that could have been sheer luck. The next one could be a killing shot. He sat up straight with a sickening thought. What if he used a tranquilizer? He groaned again, feeling sick as he came up with different possibilities. The shiver that traveled down his spine sent a shock throughout his system with the magnitude of what he could imagine.

She would be helpless.

She was smart and he trusted her to keep herself out of danger, but he knew he wasn't going to take the chance of something happening to her, any of them, either. His concerns were shattered by the ringing of the phone. He stared at it for a numb second, praying it wasn't Rebecca. *Maybe I need caller ID*, he thought as he reached for the phone.

"Benedetti."

"Hey, you. When the hell were you planning on calling Mom? She's been hounding me forever, wanting to know where you've been."

"Missed you too, Mitchell," he replied with a laugh. "Sorry. I've had a really tied-up week." *If you only knew.* "So, what's going on back east?"

Mitchell dragged in an excited breath. "You are never going to believe this, but are you sitting down? Mom is dating!"

Bram sat up. "What? Our sweet, cuss-like-a-sailor mother is dating?"

"That's the one. She's got some architect wrapped around her finger, and she doesn't cuss around him. She's Miss Congeniality."

"Holy cow!" Bram leaned onto the arm of the couch. "Is she serious?" His brow pulled down a little with worry.

"I don't know yet, but she's having the time of her life. He's been taking her all over town, introducing her to some really important people. She's out every weekend, and she never calls when she's going to be late."

"Is this what it feels like to raise kids?" Bram muttered with a wry touch of humor.

"I think it's damn close. So, are you going to talk to her about it?"

"Hell no!" Bram laughed at the absurdity. "If she's having a good time, and I don't want to know what the definition of that is, and she's happy, then let her be."

"I was afraid you'd say that," Mitchell said with a disappointed groan.

"Leave her alone. She doesn't need two grown sons ruining whatever is left of her life." He frowned when he spotted the flier again. That rock was still in his gut.

"Okay, but I did warn you."

"Duly noted. Thanks. So, anything else going on to warn me about?" He listened with half an ear as Mitch talked about the Cardinals and the year's lineup. They made tentative plans to get together for the holidays and check out their mother's new beau. By the time he hung up, his frown had deepened. He couldn't repel the chill that had filled him when he had first found the flier.

He raked a hand down his face. How was he going to keep Selene from seeing it? They were all over town. He jumped when the phone rang again. He needed to see Selene, to touch her, to hold her. To know she was safe. The second ring of the phone stopped him in mid-planning on doing all of that.

"Benedetti."

"Bram! I found you." His mood deflated faster than a popped balloon.

"Hello, Rebecca. What do you want?" he asked with a barely concealed snarl.

"That's not a nice greeting for a friend, is it?" she cooed.

He didn't answer her. "What do you want? I was on my way out the door."

"Always the busy man. Where were you going?"

"Why?" She had triggered his suspicions. She was being way too friendly. Usually the first warning signs to something she was scheming.

"I thought you might like to meet for lunch, to talk."

His eyes closed as his stomach churned. "You're here?"

She giggled softly. "Of course, silly. I came by the hospital, and this really nice blonde told me how to reach you." She paused, and he could almost hear the gears turning. *Conniving bitch.*

"You know, she was really nice, but I don't think she likes me very much," she said, clearly pouting. He knew that would have grated on Rebecca. She believed everyone should like her.

His free hand clenched. "What did you say to her?"

Her voice was full of innocence. "I introduced myself to her. What's wrong with that?"

Suddenly he felt the world tilt under his feet. Rebecca was Mrs. Benedetti to everyone.

* * * *

Selene sat in her office for hours after issuing a stunning command to not be disturbed. Priss had looked at her like she'd grown fangs, and maybe she had. She had a stack of reports and documents that needed her signature from her absence, and it helped keep her mind off Bram's wife. His wife!

She snarled under her breath, cursing him as she signed another page. No wonder he hadn't wanted to know her. At least she'd discovered he was faithful. She slashed another page as the thought brought no comfort.

Finding the raven-haired, doe-eyed woman at Priss' counter had been unexpected as she had calmly asked for Dr. Benedetti, and Selene being the kind and unsuspecting woman that she was, tried to help. Selene patted herself on the back for her show of self-restraint when she'd introduced herself as Mrs. Benedetti, Bram's estranged wife. She'd wanted to stake claim and bounce the interloping woman out on her ass, but instead she'd kept her smile plastered in place as her pressure rose a degree for every word the woman had spoken.

Oh, she'd been so disappointed to have missed him at the hospital, she'd said. He was such a dedicated doctor, she'd always known to look there first. Selene could only smile and nod as his wife had gone on and on...and on.

She stabbed at another sheet. God, she sure could pick 'em and sweet Roman had gone and put ideas in Bram's head. Personally she'd let Morgan tear him apart and keep score.

Morgan, nothing! She wanted to tear him apart.

A sharp knock stopped her ranting train. "What?" she yelled at the door without looking up.

"Selene?" The subject of her tirades poked his head in.

"I knew it was you. Where's your wife?" she snapped.

"I need to talk to you," he stated.

"No, you don't. She painted it all very well. Go to your office and do whatever you came to do. Or go home. It's your day off," she reminded him, reaching for more papers.

She bristled when he stepped in, ignoring her anger. He closed the door and locked it before she could order him out. "Selene, she's not my wife. We've been divorced for over a year and a half."

She laughed a derisive sound. "She doesn't know that. Her story is you're separated and talking reconciliation. Is that why you've kept a distance?" she demanded, anger and pain dripping from her words. "I trusted you, Bram."

His eyes narrowed at the attack. "You did that of your own free will."

She threw up her hands as she met his stare with a glare of her own. "Sorry, forgot. You're the innocent bystander to my life. I thought we were heading somewhere. I guess I was wrong. Go to hell!" She surged from behind her desk, needing to escape, but his arms captured her, stilling her attempt, if not her anger.

"I found something today that you need to see." He pulled a folded page from his rear pocket and opened it to lay on her desk. "Look. We've got bigger problems than Rebecca."

Her gaze bore holes into him for several seconds before finally drifting to the page. "Oh God." She gasped as her lungs gave out. "That's me."

"I know. Whoever it is, they are definitely after you."

This time when he tightened his hold, she melted into him. "I'm so sorry."

He smiled as he kissed her cheek. "That's okay. I've already been warned about your temper and that you're emotionally imbalanced."

She leaned away to glare again, her jaw slack. "Who told you that? I'll hurt them, I swear I will."

He laughed tenderly as he cradled her. He turned to settle his butt against the desk, bringing her with him to curl into his body. His solid, warm, so enticing body. She quivered in his hold.

"Good luck. I just got off the phone with Morgan. He called when he saw the flier, wanting to know if you had seen it yet."

She wanted to do something with that stupid grin on his face, whether to kiss it or smack it she didn't know yet, but something.

"Damn brothers," she muttered into his chest.

"I have one; I can trade one for one, but Mitchell's a big baby. You'd smear him across the state." He tilted her head, studying her with tender, dark caramel eyes. His voice dropped a few notches, a vibration that hummed through her body. "I didn't lie to you, Selene. Rebecca is a brat who never grew up. She plays for toys, and she lost her favorite one."

"You." He nodded. She felt his thumbs rubbing her through her clothes. She was turning into a puddle right there. "Where is she?"

"On the next plane out of here to wherever. I don't care," he told her. "I just spent an hour putting it in small words for her over lunch. There is no Rebecca in my world any longer. She wasn't happy, but she's not my problem."

A bubble of happiness lifted Selene, and she knew she was starting to smile again. It was reflected in his gaze.

She lifted a finger to poke into his chest. "And us?"

His arms snuggled her tight once more. "Going to your place for steak, I hope."

She searched his face, replaying his earlier words. "You said *we* have a problem?"

"I'm not about to let you do something about this alone. You almost died a few days ago. What happens if he gets to you? Finds you?" His head shake was adamant. "No way."

She couldn't hide the shudder that wracked her body. "Good point." She looked up at him. "I guess we need to figure out who this is and stop him for good."

She felt heat pool in her stomach when he brushed his thumb against her bottom lip. "Morgan said he'll be by tonight to talk about it." She could only nod. He'd turned her into a pile of mush, incapable of speech.

He tilted her up, seeking her gaze, but he didn't kiss her. He whispered against her skin as he marked her with a long, thorough swipe of his tongue on her throat.

"I am really liking that," he told her with a gentle nip, his voice vibrant and alive.

"Why won't you kiss me?" she wondered hungry and confused.

His face was calm, even though the depth of his desire glittered like fireworks in his gaze. "Because if I kiss you now, after what we've shared, I won't be able to stop, and I'm not ready to be your mate." He shook his head, adding, "Roman put it very succinctly. He's not the type you take lightly." He touched her mouth again before she could say anything.

He leaned in to whisper seductively into her ear. "Don't doubt that I want you. I want to make love to you all night. I want to feel your hands, your lips, hear your cries of passion. I've ached for you, dreamed of you." He ground his hips into her quickly for emphasis, even as his breathing became labored. "But I understand more each day. When I make love to you, when I cherish you the way I want to, the way I need to, you will have your mate."

She curled into his shoulder in acceptance. "Bram, I'm patient. I already have more than I could have ever hoped for."

He leaned close again, his breath hot where it flowed over her skin. "I do want another marking lesson, though. I was wondering, have you ever had your thigh marked?" His laugh was purely male when she shivered and moaned with delighted anticipation.

"You're evil, Bram Benedetti. Plain evil," she whimpered. His laughter filled the confines of her office for several minutes.

That evening, Bram answered the cabin door while she changed into jeans and a regular shirt. She'd been floating all afternoon after the episode in her office. He'd not only marked her neck but several inches below her blouse collar also. God, if he kept it up, she was going to burst into a walking body of flames!

She knew at some point they would mate, make love, and then there would be relief from these damnable urges that were driving her crazy. There had to be. She could go on with her life, and this insistent nagging of her body would finally be shut up. At least, that's what she prayed would happen. Or did it stop? What if the attraction didn't go away? Her eyes widened. What if it got stronger?

She knew how the body worked, what chemicals caused what impulses in the brain, but what if after they had sex it really didn't stop? What if this craving to possess and be possessed didn't go away?

Roman was the only one of the pack who was mated, but he'd fallen in love with Del. She froze where she stood in the bathroom, her brush held in midair as shock ripped through her. Was she supposed to fall in love? Would she love him? She stared hard at her reflection. Did she already love him?

It would be so easy to say that she did. She did care for him. He'd been there and proven himself over and over for her. But was love really necessary? Mating was, well, mating. Wasn't it? She knew Morgan had had a few discreet nights in a woman's company. So obviously love wasn't necessary for a mate, but he hadn't chosen one of those women for his life mate, either. So Morgan had sex. Selene hadn't. Big deal. She wasn't the last walking virgin. She couldn't be.

Maybe that was the problem. Maybe if she took a man to bed it would alleviate... She gagged over the sink.

She sucked several calming breaths, catching her wan reflection in the mirror. Okay, she got the hint. It was Bram or nothing. Back to square one.

So, if that was true, was she in love with him? She knew she wanted him physically. She wanted him so much that she burst into heat when he walked into the room, and it was getting continually stronger. She thought of his tenderness, his warmth. He was protective of her, of that she was sure, or he wouldn't have included himself in the hunt for the man who had shot her twice.

She closed her eyes and remembered how he had stared at her when she had shown her secret to him. The shock had turned to awe, his careful observations had turned to joy as he'd held her. Even when she'd been too weak to change, he'd stayed with her.

Her gaze opened slowly when she realized what she'd found. She held it close, the uncertainty of the future holding her in a death grip. The warmth of the feeling was new and raw. She wasn't ready. She couldn't face it yet. Too much was still left out there, too many unanswered questions, and so many threats. Knowing how she felt, really deep down for Bram, was a gift in itself.

Her frozen hand moved over her hair distractedly as the truth of her discovery filled her, but the brush froze over her hair when the phone rang. At Morgan's shout she dropped her brush in the sink and ran for the front room.

"What is it?" she asked, gasping and sliding to a stop.

"Del had the baby! Eight pounds, two ounces, and all boy!" Morgan was grinning as he lifted the phone again. "That's great, Roman. How is she doing? Yeah, and you? Lots of love, man. We'll see you as soon as we get this poacher problem cleared up." Morgan's laugh was deep as he nodded. "Yeah, yeah. Wait until Mom and Dad see him." He laughed again, then said, "Don't even think about it; you have a family. Man, I never thought I'd say that about any of us. Watch your tongue, you have a son now." His gaze tripped toward Selene. "Sure, hold on. Selene, he wants to say hi." He held out the phone.

"Hiya," she said, grinning happily for her brother.

"Hey, little stuff. Are things settling down for you?"

She grinned wider at his pet name for her. "They're starting to," she said.

"Well, if he gives you any more problems, let me know. I think we connected, more than Morgan did, anyway." His voice lowered as he told her with a chuckle, "I think I scared him a little."

"Oh, Roman, go be a daddy, you knucklehead." She buried her face in her hand before she laughed outright at him. "Love to you and Del."

"Back at you, sis. See you real soon. Bye." And he hung up.

She turned around, but it was just her and Bram in the room. "Where'd Morgan go?" She replaced the phone.

"I think he went to see if there was anyone outside." Bram didn't have to say Morgan was acting edgy. She'd seen it already when he'd arrived. Bram walked to stand in front of her. "You're real close, your family, aren't you?"

"Very. Kind of a mutual admiration society." She felt her smile answering his grin.

"I can see how that could be." He traced a finger across her jaw, and her heart thundered into her ribs. His voice was low and sensuous as he searched her face. "Selene, do you remember what I said earlier about kissing you?"

Her gaze collided with those lips. The ones that belonged to him. The lips that she wanted to taste again, needed to feel with heated passion as he... "Yes," she said breathily, barely able to stay standing under the onslaught of need.

He swept her into the circle of his arms, a ring of fire that blazed around her. "Please, tell me this is real," he managed to say. "I've thought of little else all day. The wanting is killing me, but I won't take from you." His desire was so close to the surface, his aching rush was colliding with hers.

The warmth of his body flowed over her, his scent covering her, her senses coming alive in his hold. She pressed herself into him in comfort and felt his arms tighten, like he didn't want to let her go. She lifted her head, her nose grazing his throat, and watched as he swallowed, barely under control.

Impulsively, she swept her tongue up the shaved side of his throat and felt the vibrated reaction up and down her body where they touched.

"God, is that what it feels like for you when I do it?" He panted in needy wonder seconds later.

She pressed her lips against him where he curled over her, breathing hard and trembling. As she spoke, she felt his body's strengthening reaction again. "I don't know how to explain it, but it's the best mark I've ever received." She teased him with her breath, her voice, her lips, and her tongue until he quivered in her hold.

"No wonder your kisses..." He stopped. His gaze was penetrating as they locked on each other, a secret message passing between them. "You make me feel more alive than I've ever felt in my whole life."

It was on her tongue. How much she wanted him. How much he meant to her. She wanted him to take her to bed and let her forget that outside her door, someone was lying in wait for her. She wanted him.

"Sorry to break this up, but our problem is here, and he means business."

Bram and Selene jumped apart like two guilty children as they faced Morgan, his expression enraged as he stood before them covered in dirt. He caught Selene's gaze, his concern and fear for her right on the surface. He held in his hand a new trap, stronger than the old style they'd been destroying, and new bait. A very effective bait.

He held a picture of her.

Chapter Eleven

Selene was grateful that Bram had dropped a hand to wrap around her waist. He was able to hold her up when her knees changed to water and her legs began to collapse beneath her.

"Oh God. He did see me." Her stomach flipped at her carelessness. The photograph was a picture of her leaving the hospital that afternoon.

Morgan's tone was ominous. "I think he's known for some time and that's why he's been trying to catch one of us. He never figured out the traps wouldn't work."

"But why would anyone do that?" Bram asked, still holding her close.

Morgan shot him an impatient look. "Think. If you had a million-dollar wolf, what would you do? If you could produce a bloodline of self-healing warriors, could duplicate what we are?"

Bram released a harsh breath, raking a hand down his face. "Damn, I didn't even think of it that way."

She pointed with a shaking hand at the picture. "Where did you find that?"

"I found it tacked up on the tree the trap was anchored to. It's a warning. He knows we've been destroying the traps and he knows, at least, of you."

"Can't we confront him? There has to be a way to protect all of you," Bram insisted.

Morgan dropped the trap unceremoniously on the porch, slamming the door on it. "And tell him what?"

he demanded, snarling. "Um, sorry, but could you please quit trying to plunk one of us in the butt?" Morgan shook his head derisively. "Somehow I don't think that's going to work."

Morgan fell into a chair with a dark, cross look as Bram and Selene took over the couch.

"This is my fault," she whispered, heartbroken. "I should have been more careful."

Bram supported her chin with a finger. "What's done is done. We've already been over that."

She nodded once. "You're right. One thing at a time."

Morgan braced his weight on an elbow, a little calmer. But not by much. "So what do we do, folks? We can't let him continue to trap; he's hurting the small game. I've smelled the blood of death more times than I want to remember when he misses us, and I know I'm not letting him get to any of us."

"I'm not either," Bram said vehemently. "I can go to the police and take in the trap as evidence."

Selene laid a gentle hand on Bram's knee. "I know you mean well. We've already done that. Morgan even threw some of his Forestry weight around to get more people involved. It didn't go anywhere. Wolves don't live here. We do."

"I hate feeling helpless," Bram admitted.

"I know," she told him. She looked at Morgan. There was only one way. "We have to do this ourselves, and he can't survive."

"You mean...?" Bram swallowed, a gray color taking over his features.

"Bram, he knows," she stressed. "Our secret is sacred." She grazed a tender hand down his face as she stood. "It's time this was over. Two years is too long."

Bram stood next to her, and she felt blessed with his support. "Then I'm coming with you. I can shoot, and at least I can talk when you two can't."

"He has a point," Morgan agreed.

She whipped around abruptly, facing Bram. "No! You can't. This is too dangerous. If he knows what we are, he won't stop." She caught the fire in his earth-brown gaze and waited for several heart-stopping seconds.

"Morgan, I need to speak to Selene." His voice was soft, but there was a powerful undercurrent she'd never heard before.

Morgan was up and gone before she could blink.

"What are you thinking? I won't let you do this; you can't endanger yourself! I won't let you!" she cried, frightened for him in a new, and very disturbing, way.

He lifted his hands to cradle her face, gentle even though his voice was thick and fierce. "But I'm supposed to let you and Morgan trot out that door as if everything is going to be fine? You're going out to stop a man, to kill a man, who wants to own you. Who, for whatever reason, has no problem with you being injured...or dead." His lips thinned. "And I'm supposed to accept that?"

"Look at it from my point of view," she pleaded.

"I am, and I know I'm not going to let you leave and do this alone." His gaze narrowed as his head lowered. "You see, Selene, he can't own you. He can't have you in any way. You are mine! You are mine to protect. You are mine for every reason I draw breath."

His kiss was harsh and possessive, slashing with the finality of his decision. She shook uncontrollably as heat rose and flared, consuming them both equally.

She was weak when he finally pulled away, her eyelids fluttering in the aftermath.

His gaze had not changed, and if anything he looked more determined. It gave her a chill along her spine. "Selene, you are mine," he repeated, albeit at least a little gentler. "We will find a way out of this, for all of our sakes. And then," he said, his voice lowering to a depth that caressed over her ears, "we will discuss us." He lifted his head, standing tall. "Morgan! Let's take care of this."

The shiver that shot over her body had nothing to do with Bram's closeness.

* * * *

Two nights later, Bram was no less concerned or less enraged over the situation this unnamed poacher had created. He'd gone to the police to let them know that one of their own, one of the respected people of the community, was being threatened, and still he didn't get more than a bare head nod of curiosity.

Now, because of that, he was sitting in Selene's living room, cleaning his father's rifle and ensuring he had sufficient ammunition. In his heart, he didn't want to have to hurt a bug, but if he was the only thing between Selene and capture, torture, and death, then what choice did he have? He would protect her and her family with his last breath if he had no other option. It had come down to that.

It had hit him with the force of a two-ton truck standing in her living room two nights before, staring into her eyes as she fought to keep him safe. She was his, in every way a man was supposed to protect and cherish his woman. His wife. His mate.

His mouth thinned as he sighted the rifle one more time. Very little had been said in the two days since. He had tried to keep it under the surface, his anger, his love. He still had hours to work, and no one could know what they were doing tonight. They were going to be hunting the hunter.

He barely looked up when Morgan came in, closing the door behind him. "Any word from Selene?" Morgan asked. His voice was level and calm, but Bram could sense his anxiety and determination. Neither man was happy with the plan that they had worked out, but it had been worked to the barest of errors, and it relied on Selene. It was tearing Bram apart.

He grunted a negative, resetting the safety and looking up. He wasn't alarmed anymore at the feral light in Morgan's eyes. Now that Bram knew and had been accepted as one of them, Morgan and Bram had reached an understanding. Morgan had relaxed his inner spirit. It showed now through his dark gray gaze with a heat of the hunt that was barely contained.

Bram understood. He didn't want to be waiting here. He wanted to be after the man who was threatening his woman, her life, and her family.

It didn't take long for Selene to arrive, slipping in and quickly grabbing a robe that Morgan offered. She brushed her hair with a steady hand, but Bram could see the hesitation in her gaze. She didn't want him out there any more than he wanted her involved.

"Did you find him?" Morgan asked.

"Yes, and he saw me." She turned and faced Bram. "He's camped close by, about three miles." Bram didn't even flinch when he heard thunder in the distance.

"Fine, then the first step is done. Selene, you stay here," Bram commanded.

She shook her head. "I can't. Bram, he's not alone."

"Great. How many?" Morgan said.

Both men jumped when a cell phone rang. Bram hesitated seeing it wasn't the hospital, but answered after the third ring, a chilled feeling filling his soul.

"Oh, thank God!" sobbed Rebecca. He bit his anger; she'd intruded one time too many in his life.

"What?" he snarled, his pent-up energy growing.

There was a loud, shocked cry, then suddenly a male voice came across the phone. "Good. I'm glad she was right, it will make this easier." It was a deep voice, no one he recognized. "You have something I want."

"Who is this?" he demanded.

"That isn't important. I want to trade."

"I don't know what you're talking about! I don't know her!" Bram said, gritting his teeth. He flinched when Rebecca screamed in the background.

"You were saying?" the evil voice taunted.

"What do you want?" Bram asked, forcing a calm he didn't feel.

"A trade. This woman for the wolf," the deep voice said. Bram heard no other noises, no indications of where he was. "She was here. Send her, and I will give up the princess."

"She's not here," he lied. His heart tripped over the man's words. He did know the truth about Selene.

"You have thirty minutes." And the phone went dead.

"He has Rebecca," Bram said hollowly, disconnecting the signal.

Morgan growled low. "Why would he hold a captive?"

"He wants to trade," Bram replied. Morgan hissed a breath. "He's out of luck." He strode to pick up the rifle. "What direction is the trail, Selene? We need to pick it up before the rain hits."

"I'm coming with you." Her voice and expression were emotionless.

"Selene," Morgan insisted, but she changed without bothering to answer and headed for the door. She looked once over her shoulder, directly at Bram, and he knew what she was going to do. He cursed roundly. "Do your thing, Morgan. We're on," he said as he headed out the door, following her pale coat as she streaked for the trees.

Bram followed her quickly, her light color his only beacon in the shadowed woods. A cloud cover obliterated any hope of moonlight. Morgan followed close at his heels.

How had the poacher gotten to Rebecca? She was supposed to have gone home two days ago. How did he even know who she was? Who was this man?

Thirty minutes later, his phone rang again. He muffled the sound, then answered calmly.

"You have one chance to save this one," the man on the other end warned him.

Bram had stopped and saw that both Selene and Morgan were listening. "What do you want?" Bram asked him.

"Come to the crushed embankment. She will know. You will find this one after I have the wolf." The line went dead again.

"Damn!" he cursed softly. He repeated it for their benefit. Morgan sneezed. It sounded vaguely like a curse. "Yeah, me too, pal. He's not going to get what he thinks he is." He thought for a minute. "He doesn't know we've left yet!" he crowed softly. They had time on their side. "How close is the rain?"

Morgan dropped a paw over his nose. "That's not good," Bram murmured. "But then again... I have a new plan." He knelt on the ground and drew it out. The two wolves looked at each other, then at him. Bram looked directly at Selene. She was going to be bait. Again. They needed more time, and drawing the man away from his own plan was the only thing they had in their favor.

"Please, please be careful," he begged her.

She moved forward and raised a paw, resting it over his heart, and then like a flash of the growing lightning, she was gone.

"Can you get the trail again?" Morgan dropped his nose and started off, looking over his shoulder to keep track of Bram. The darkness was heavy as the storm began to move in. The moisture was building, and he knew they had less than fifteen minutes before the rain was going to hit. They had to be close enough to get to Rebecca, then get to Selene. The whole time he ran to keep pace with Morgan, he silently prayed to keep Selene safe.

He remained on Morgan's tail and sensed as he slowed. He followed suit, crouching low. "Is he still there?" Bram asked, peering through the trees. It was black as ink, and he couldn't see any more than a few feet in front of himself.

Morgan shook his furry head, stepping cautiously. Bram pushed branches out of the way with a careful hand. He could barely see Rebecca tied up next to a tent. She was wearing the same outfit she had worn on the day of her visit, and she looked absolutely terrified.

He circled the encampment, walking up behind her when he was satisfied she was alone. He clamped a hand over her mouth. "Shh! It's me. Don't make a sound. I'm going to untie you." She nodded quickly. He fought with her bonds, finally working her hands free. He helped her sit up, then told her, "Follow him out. He'll take you to a safe place, but he has to come to help me. We will return for you. Okay?"

"Are you nuts?" she tried to screech, but her throat was dry, and all that emerged was a hoarse croak.

"Rebecca! There is another woman he's after! He will kill her! For once, this isn't about you." He snarled through a hard jaw. He shook her quickly by the shoulders when her mouth popped open. "Just do it.

The rain is about to hit." He looked over his shoulder at Morgan.

She tried to scream. "It's a freaking wolf!"

"And he's going to save you! Now go!" He lifted her to her feet and shoved her toward the tree line. "Be quick, Morgan. Please."

Morgan started off at a lope but stopped and growled. "Damn it! Rebecca, go! You're pissing him off!"

She paled but did as she was told, stumbling stiffly after the darker-than-night shadow in front of her. Bram had to wait five, ten, fifteen minutes, until he thought he would cry with anguished worry. The rain hit when Morgan cleared the trees. Their eyes locked, and they turned with one purpose.

Morgan's ears pricked, and then even Bram heard it. The lamenting call of a wolf. Bram knew that call from his heart to his very soul.

"Damn it! He's found her!"

His lungs were hurting with strain, and the rushed trek through the woods. That sound wrenched him to his soul. Morgan picked up the pace, Bram fighting to keep him in his line of vision. Morgan's darker coat was a lot harder to keep ahead of him through the rain.

He almost stumbled when he heard a shot fired. It had been close. He had no idea how much of his approach was covered by the rain and thunder. Lord knew he was making enough noise, but he couldn't help it.

She howled again, and she still sounded strong. "Thank heavens! Where is she, Morgan? I can't see shit!"

Morgan stopped a few feet ahead of Bram, scenting the ground and the air, and Bram heard the low growl emanating from him. "It's all right. We'll get him." He watched as Morgan dropped his nose, then growled. "He's close? Which way?"

Morgan faced toward Bram's left side. "All right, I'm working blind, but I'll see if I can get close." When Morgan started to slink to the right, Bram stopped. "Hey." Morgan looked over his shoulder. "Be careful." Morgan blinked, then started off again.

It took him several minutes of slow, blind walking while a hard, cold rain drenched him. He worked with his ears more than his eyes, fighting for anything that would lead him to them. To her. Three steps, eight steps, ten, then he heard him. Cursing. That was a good sign. Something wasn't going according to plan.

He slowed even more, squinting through the dark. He swiped water from his face angrily as he crouched, listening. The other man was cursing the weather. Did she get away? Then he heard a whimper, and his heart slid to his shoes with the weight of an anvil.

Bram rolled around a tree and could see him, barely. The other man's red flannel shirt was plastered to him and was as dark as the night. He didn't look like a mountain man, not even in the pitch black of a rain soaked night. His hair was too short, and he was clean-shaven. Bram inched closer, his rifle aimed at the man standing over the pale wolf on the ground. He slid the safety off with a noiseless motion.

"Back away from the wolf!" Bram shouted as he steadied the rifle. The man stood and turned to him, apparently unable to find Bram in the rain and darkness. The rain was slowing, but it was still enough to cause a sheet of murkiness between them.

"Who's there?" the other man yelled.

"I've come for the wolf," Bram said. "Step away."

"She's mine!" the other man yelled. "I've hunted this one for two years."

Bram swallowed. How long had he known? "Why? Wolves are endangered!" he snarled. "You are breaking the law, poaching on protected land."

The other man actually snorted. "So what? I am the law. And she's going to make my ass rich!" There was a flash of lightning overhead and Bram blinked, blinded by the flash. A fork of power hit somewhere close by. The stench of ozone burned his nostrils for a long second.

He wasn't prepared for what happened next. There was a glint of a pistol in the one flash lightning. As the report ricocheted through his ears, he felt ripping pain as he tumbled backward. Morgan landed squarely on the other man's frame, knocking him down with a devastating growl and the fierce strength of unrelenting jaws. There was a snap of bone, then silence as the man stilled beneath the wolf's weight.

Bram felt rain on his face lying in the soaked leaves and couldn't remember how he got there.

"Hey, Doc. You okay?" Morgan was asking him, slapping his cheek.

His eyes opened and blinked. "Hurts." Morgan immediately began to look him over.

"Where? Can you move anything?" Morgan ran his hands down Bram's arms.

"Selene? Where is she?" He gasped. God, did he hurt.

"She'll be fine. He stunned her. Where did he hit you?" Morgan asked again, an impatient question.

Bram lifted his hand; his arm felt all right. Then he took a breath, and his last thought was that he was going to die before he blacked out.

Chapter Twelve

"Come on, Bram. Pull through," Selene pleaded under her breath as she finished packing the wound to stop the bleeding. "I owe you this one."

He was out cold, her bed put to service as an operating table one more time. An ambulance was on the way, called as soon as they'd walked into her home. The bullet had gone deep, a .38 at close range, but by some miracle, hadn't hit anything important, lodging beneath his lungs and ribcage. She took a shaky breath, wishing that she could give him her gift to heal. She rested a hand on his chest, willing him to live, to be whole.

She was refusing to succumb to the shakes that her ordeal had brought on her, refusing to acknowledge how close things had gotten. How close Bram had come to dying, how close she had come to being caught. She sucked in needed oxygen to find some thread of balanced sanity. One catastrophe at a time.

Morgan explained after Bram had passed out that he had worked to make her stable enough to get Bram home between the two of them. Nothing else mattered. Not the other woman, not the dead man. Nothing. He had to live. She blinked scalding tears away, kneeling at the bedside with him.

"Selene, the chief is here. They found Markson," Morgan said from over her shoulder. "I'll stay with him." She nodded carefully. She still ached and was filthy from the elbows up. Bram needed to be taken to the hospital.

She took a steadying breath to hide the remaining adrenaline-pushed shivers when Morgan drifted a finger down her cheek. "Don't worry. You know what to tell them. Rebecca is still hysterical. Something about a wolf," he told her with a mocking rise of his lip, the understanding immediate between them.

She nodded. She hoped she had the capacity to talk in the next three minutes. She glanced at the wall of her family, immediately finding a store of strength in seeing them all together. Someone had put her painting up on the wall. She knew it could have only been Bram.

She didn't even blink an eye seeing five strangers in her home, a secluded home that until that night no one had known of. Now half of Bend knew where she lived. She took another steadying breath. One thing at a time.

"Chief?" she said, getting his attention.

He caught her gaze and then quickly dropped it, a guilty air hanging about him. "Dr. Aiza. I am truly sorry that this happened," Chief Swarenson began. "You have no idea how badly my department, or myself, feels for not taking Dr. Benedetti's warnings seriously. No one ever saw the reports Markson was taking. I wouldn't have been surprised if he shredded them. There was nothing in the computers, either."

She met his apologetic stare with an equally cool one. "I hope that your department will understand if someone suspects this kind of activity in the future that it will be followed up on. Both myself and Morgan placed complaints over a year ago with your department about the poacher situation."

"Yes," he replied, looking extremely uncomfortable in having that pointed out. A lack of reports didn't make his department innocent in the situation.

"He kidnapped not only Dr. Benedetti's ex-wife, but attempted to kill him in the process of him saving her," she gave him a superior glacier stare, "when your department neglected to take proper control of the situation."

He cleared his throat. "Do you happen to know who or what he was actually after?"

"I'm not entirely sure." She made a disgusted sound in her throat. "He was delusional, as we found out tonight. He said something about how he was going to get rich because of a wolf he had found."

Chief Swarenson scratched his head. "But there aren't any wolves out here."

She crossed her arms. "I'm aware of that." Her gaze shot over the chief's shoulder as the expected ambulance pulled up. When Jeffrey pushed through the door, she pointed to her bedroom, giving directions as they walked by. She faced the chief again. "I'm going with them to the hospital. Is there anything else?"

"No, I don't guess so." He hung his head, well aware of how badly his department had fouled up. Letting a deputy hunt uncontrolled on protected property, kidnapping, attempted murder. They were in it up to their necks, and he knew it.

She bit off the snarl that was perched right beneath the surface. She wanted to shred them all for their incompetence, but she was still running high on adrenaline and anger. It would fade with time. And with knowing Bram would be all right.

She turned at the sound of the EMTs coming from the bedroom. "Jeffrey, give me a minute. I'm riding in with you."

He looked at Bram on the stretcher and nodded in answer. "He's stable. You did nice work." Then they carried out the man who owned her heart, body, and soul to the open doors of the ambulance.

* * * *

Bram blinked, gritty eyes sliding closed wearily. He was alive. The last thing he remembered was Morgan telling him Selene was alive and going to be all right. He slowly opened his eyes, very gradually becoming aware of his surroundings. He heard the beep of the heart monitor, felt the inserted IV needle in the back of his hand with the tight, uncomfortable medical tape. How long had he been here?

He swiveled his head, taking it all in. There were flowers and a few cards propped up across the room. He had been there for quite a while, if that was any indication. Was he in Bend? Had they sent him somewhere? The room was relatively plain, a single private. He wished his mind wasn't so fuzzy. He wanted to remember.

He felt a tingle down his neck, felt...something, and rolled his head in the other direction. He found her, watching him, quietly sitting in a chair at his bedside. Beautiful gray eyes soft with love and lips that trembled wildly with restrained emotions.

"Hi," she whispered.

"Hi," he croaked. He swallowed. She gave him some water to sip and he felt considerably better. "How long?"

"Six days."

"Why?" His brow tightened.

"You had a really high fever for two days." She brushed loose hair out of his eyes. When she scraped over his beard growth, he realized she wasn't fibbing on the truth. "Your mother is here. She's staying at your place. Do you want to see her?"

He shook his head, feeling groggy but fighting it. "Not yet." He lifted his hand, reaching for hers. "How are you?" His fingers twined with hers, and he felt a surge of healing warmth.

"A wreck," she said, smiling through her tears. "But I improved greatly two minutes ago."

"Morgan?"

"Fine. He's at home right now. I'll call him in a bit to tell him you're awake. He'll be glad."

"I don't remember. Is everything over?" He was trying, but was drawing a blank.

"Yes, Bram. It's over," she whispered. She leaned close to breathe a warm caress against his ear. "He's dead. You didn't shoot him," she said when he clenched his hand over hers. "And Rebecca was rescued by the police. I won't blame you if you get mad, but we had to choose. Her or you. She stayed the night in the rain."

He chuckled. Rebecca was the last person he was concerned about right at that moment. "I'm not mad." He lifted a hand to brush against warm skin, feeling the silken smoothness of it and reveling in that touch. "I'm not strong enough right now, but you know what's going to happen when I get out, don't you?"

He smiled when her cheeks flushed lightly. "What, Bram?"

"We need to take a long, temporary leave."

"Why?" she asked, mildly confused.

He pulled her down to nip at her ear. "For our honeymoon." He breathed against her. "That is, if you still want me, if you can say yes."

He found a light glowing in her gaze when she straightened at his shoulder, a primal need that he felt deeply and wanted to answer. She bent over and offered her answer, licking the sensitive side of his neck. "Consider yourself marked," she murmured heatedly for him.

He moaned, his eyes drifting shut as sensations bombarded him, reawakening him with a powerful kick that was stronger than the best coffee. "Promise me you will never forget how to do that."

"Not in a million years," she replied, a glowing smile proving she meant it.

"Ahem, can I interrupt?" Bram smiled at the voice, his eyes opening once more to the whiteness of the room and the owner of the voice. He saw Selene sit up with a guilty blush as a man entered the room wearing a firefighter T-shirt and jeans.

"Mitchell." Bram groaned.

"Glad to see you too," his brother said. Bram held her tight when she tried to move away. "Mom called and said you did something stupid and stepped in front of a bullet."

"Trying to save the trees," Bram said with a joking twist of his lips. "What brings you out this way?"

"I was called out for the storms. Those lightning strikes set off some corridor fires. I would've been here sooner," he explained.

Bram nodded and understood. Duty first. "Well, I guess it's good fortune you're here first, then. I want you to meet my fiancée. This is Dr. Selene Aiza." Mitchell had neared to greet her, accepting her hand.

Mitchell started. "Seriously? Wow, Mom never said."

Selene bit her lip. It was nice watching the way she blushed. He hoped he was able to do that to her for many long years to come. "He asked right before you came in," she replied.

Mitchell smiled warmly. "I see. Got ya before you could run." He winked at her easily. Bram noticed the way his brother's gaze enjoyed Selene. He felt a hot stab of jealousy. He laid down the law quickly before it got out of hand, even if he did wholeheartedly agree and knew nothing would come of it. Bram didn't want there to be any misunderstanding.

"Mitchell, just because I'm in this bed doesn't mean I won't kick your ass. She's mine," he said with a low, grumbled threat.

Mitch raised his hands, laughing. Selene chuckled, shaking her head gently, then she clasped Bram's fingers tighter within her own.

She shot Bram a mischievous glance. "But you know what, I do have a sister."

"Really?" Mitch responded quickly, his gaze lightening with interest.

"Thought you didn't set up people?" he teased her, playing along.

She shrugged. "He's not people. He's family now. *Family* is fair game," she said with a devilish grin.

"Hey, I'm still here," Mitchell said from the edge of the bed, waving at them. Bram and Selene laughed easily, and he relaxed.

They talked for a few minutes, then Mitchell said he was going to let their mom know he was awake and left them saying he'd be around after lunch.

Bram was extremely content to simply hold Selene's hand. He licked his lips, feeling stronger by the minute. "So, how did Rebecca get tied up with Markson anyway?" he asked.

Selene settled into her chair. "From what I was told, when you and she had that little argument over lunch, Markson stepped up to offer comfort when you left. The big law type, and she fell for it."

"I'm sorry about that. I had no idea she'd go so crazy. I really thought she understood this time and was leaving." How many times was he supposed to say the same damn things before Rebecca got the message? She had thrown a classic fit, the kind he'd become immune to. Coming to Bend had only given Markson a pawn to use in his plans.

"Everyone argues," she said calmly. "From the report she gave the chief, she didn't know she was in trouble until Markson refused to take her to her hotel. It's hard to not instinctively trust someone who's supposed to be on our side."

"Yes. I can see that. She's used to getting her own way and being catered to," he agreed.

"If you want to see her..."

He shook his head. "I will call her and see her when I'm ready to. And don't worry. I'll make sure this time she understands it's over." He was done playing her games. He closed his eyes, resting for a minute. "So how long am I stuck in here?"

"Not much longer. You are doing well, and Dr. Lin said you're in great health. Which I already knew."

"You're not my doctor?" he asked, mildly surprised.

"I couldn't. I've been right here or asleep since we brought you in."

His heart warmed on those words. Her simple expression said everything about how she felt for him, but it wouldn't hurt to hear the words. So he started.

"I love you, Selene. I realized it the night you wanted to keep me away from it all. I love you for everything that you are, the incredible woman, the doctor." He lifted his hand from hers, cradling her face in a palm. His heart tripped heavily as her warmth filled him. Her eyes had drifted closed at his touch. "But especially because of what I found." Her eyes opened at the seriousness of his tone. "All my life, I've felt like I had a part of me that was lacking. Adrift. When we left to find Markson, I knew I was going to protect you until my last breath. I was going to protect all of you, and I was willing. That is what you meant, isn't it? About me being your mate?" His voice was a secretive whisper in the room.

"Yes, Bram," she replied, her voice thick with tears. "I love you, too. You are the man I've waited for, my mate, in every sense of the word."

He swallowed. "Hell, I have got to get out of here," he grumbled, searching the room for any escape. "I want to hold you so badly."

"I can do something about that," she said. He dropped his arm, and she lifted herself high to hold him close against her. His arms wrapped around her, and he felt peace. He had found his heart.

He nuzzled her ear. "So tell me something?" She nodded against his shoulder. "This ability you have, does it, you know, pass down?"

Her body shook with her light laughter. "Yes, but we have time. Dad can explain it better. He's had four of us go through it."

"Oh boy." He sighed with a smile.

About the Author

With more than fifty e-books currently to her credit and several books in print, Diana Castilleja has kept busy since she started writing professionally in late 2004.

Diana currently resides in central Texas with her husband and son. When not focusing her energy on her family and her writing, she loves to travel and haunt bookstores. She's lived in several states across the south and midwest, as well as traveling to Mexico. With moving every year or changing schools since the fourth grade to her sophomore year, she learned that reading was a fast escape. The freedom to read about anything and everything has fueled her adult imagination. She also enjoys romance, horses, and yes, still loves to read.

Visit her online at www.DianaCastilleja.com

PURPLE SWORD PUBLICATIONS
Romance and Speculative Fiction
www.purplesword.com